W9-AAD-376

> *"My instincts have saved me uncountable times during my career. I'm not going to start ignoring them now."*

Liz couldn't argue with Sam. But agreeing to let him work on the Windsor case seemed absurd when she thought about her complete physical response to him. Still, the instincts she had learned to trust were telling her to let him stay. That sending him away would be a huge mistake.

"It shouldn't be a problem to get approval for you to consult on this investigation with me," Liz told him. "Just don't forget it's *my* investigation, Broussard."

His gaze slid down her body, touching every part of her with a hot, melting look. Something dark came and went in his gaze. "I don't plan to cause you any problems, Liz."

Too late, she thought while her hammering pulse turned everything inside her hot and sensitive.

Too late.

Dear Reader,

Reconciliation. I have a soft spot for a story that brings characters back to someone they loved and lost. So, I thought, what about writing a miniseries about three couples with shared pasts? Stories where passion is intensified by memory and by deferred longing. And where better for lovers to come together again than in Reunion Square, an almost mystical enclave of quaint shops and businesses?

Three women. Three men from their pasts. Three different journeys that take us to the "ever after" part of love that was destined to be.

In the second of these books, a hot lead on a cold murder case brings Louisiana detective Sam Broussard to Oklahoma City. Although Sam knows he's never met OCPD sergeant Liz Scott, there's something familiar about the leggy redhead. As they dig into a haunting past neither remembers sharing, Sam and Liz hunt a killer bent on separating them for all eternity. And Sam has one last chance to reach across time to save the woman he's destined to love forever.

Suspensefully,

Maggie Price

THE PASSION
OF SAM BROUSSARD

Maggie Price

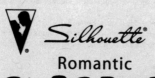

Romantic
SUSPENSE

If you purchased this book without a cover you should be aware that this book is stolen property. It was reported as "unsold and destroyed" to the publisher, and neither the author nor the publisher has received any payment for this "stripped book."

SILHOUETTE BOOKS

ISBN-13: 978-0-373-27572-4
ISBN-10: 0-373-27572-2

THE PASSION OF SAM BROUSSARD

Copyright © 2008 by Margaret Price

All rights reserved. Except for use in any review, the reproduction or utilization of this work in whole or in part in any form by any electronic, mechanical or other means, now known or hereafter invented, including xerography, photocopying and recording, or in any information storage or retrieval system, is forbidden without the written permission of the editorial office, Silhouette Books, 233 Broadway, New York, NY 10279 U.S.A.

This is a work of fiction. Names, characters, places and incidents are either the product of the author's imagination or are used fictitiously, and any resemblance to actual persons, living or dead, business establishments, events or locales is entirely coincidental.

This edition published by arrangement with Harlequin Books S.A.

® and TM are trademarks of Harlequin Books S.A., used under license. Trademarks indicated with ® are registered in the United States Patent and Trademark Office, the Canadian Trade Marks Office and in other countries.

Visit Silhouette Books at www.eHarlequin.com

Printed in U.S.A.

Books by Maggie Price

Silhouette Romantic Suspense

Prime Suspect #816
The Man She Almost Married #838
Most Wanted #948
On Dangerous Ground #989
Dangerous Liaisons #1043
Special Report #1045
  "Midnight Seduction"
Moment of Truth #1143
*Sure Bet #1263
*Hidden Agenda #1269
*The Cradle Will Fall #1276
*Shattered Vows #1335
*Most Wanted Woman #1396
**Jackson's Woman #1464
**The Passion of Sam Broussard #1502

Silhouette Bombshell

*Trigger Effect #47

Harlequin Books

The Ransom

The Coltons

Protecting Peggy

*Line of Duty
**Dates with Destiny

MAGGIE PRICE

Before embarking on a writing career, Maggie Price took a walk on the wild side and began associating with people who carry guns. Fortunately they were cops, and Maggie's career as a crime analyst with the Oklahoma City Police Department has given her the background needed to write true-to-life police procedural romances, which have won numerous accolades, including a nomination for the coveted RITA® Award.

Maggie is a recipient of a Golden Heart Award, a Career Achievement Award from *Romantic Times BOOKreviews,* a National Reader's Choice Award and a Bookseller's Best Award, all in series romantic suspense. Readers are invited to contact Maggie at 416 N.W. 8th St., Oklahoma City, OK 73102-2604, or on the Web at www.MaggiePrice.com.

To timeless love…

Prologue

He'd come to her in a dream each night for the past two weeks. His voice was low, insistent, ripe with warning. And always, the words slipped away, becoming only a hazy memory when she woke.

His blue eyes glittered down at her while his rough hands steadied her, stroking her bare flesh. She sensed he was dangerous, yet she clung to him, reveling in the sinewed, muscled feel of him between her thighs.

Ghostly moonlight broke through the clouds, seeped through the bedroom windows. Tonight, as all others, the light was too weak to illuminate his face—all she had ever seen was the intense, heated blue of his eyes. Eyes that stayed locked with hers as he took her. Possessed her.

Made her his.

All at once, the moonlight hazed over. The air went cold, bringing with it a sharp terror....

"No!"

With the scream still tearing at her throat, Elizabeth Scott shot up in bed. Her fingers clutched reflexively at the cover while she clawed her way through the slippery edges of the dream and battled the icy fear that always came back with her.

She dragged in deep gulps of the night air, knowing that the fear would soon ebb. It always did after the murky dream that began with pleasure and ended on the brink of panic.

She waited while her blood cooled and the last remnants of completion throbbed inside her. He'd spoken to her—she was sure of that—but now, as always, she couldn't pull his words from her memory. Experience had also taught her that if she slid her hands along her inner thighs there would be no trace of him left there. How could there be when his presence had been only a dream? A dream during which she could swear she'd engaged in hot, passionate sex with a man she didn't know but whose body was as familiar to her as her own.

She'd given up denying she wanted the apparition she'd tagged Dream Lover. In truth, she lusted for the man whose face she had never fully glimpsed.

"Who are you?" she whispered and dragged a pillow over her face in a failed attempt to block her thoughts.

Suspicion she was going bonkers wasn't a quality

prized by a police detective who had recently snagged a transfer to the Oklahoma City P.D.'s new cold case office. Her assignment involved uncountable hours spent poring over individual case files yellowed with age and filled with hopelessness. Ferreting out leads that had lain dormant for years required a clear mind and absolute concentration. How could she analyze facts and unearth leads when all logic was slowly eroding from her life?

"Holy hell," she muttered against the pillow.

She was convinced the dream was payback. Some cosmic retribution for hurting the man she'd been so sure she loved. And had planned to marry…twice!

After her second attempt at walking down the aisle failed, her engagement went south. That same night, Dream Lover first appeared, sweeping her away in a fantasy far more erotic than anything she'd experienced while awake.

"Dammit!" Liz flung the pillow away, kicked aside the tangled sheets and rose. Jerking on her robe, she headed downstairs and stalked across her tenth-floor loft. The hardwood floor felt cool against her bare feet as she stood before the glass door that opened off the balcony. Outside, the sky was a dark, cobalt-blue bowl studded with diamonds. It would be hours before dawn broke over Reunion Square. Hours before Liz was due at the police department, her first day back since her life turned upside down and Dream Lover made his initial visit.

She clenched her fists, hating the sense she was

losing her grip on the control over her life she'd worked so hard to gain. That's what came from having been abandoned when she was a week old, then flung into the chaos of foster care. She *liked* sitting in the driver's seat, steering her life in the direction she chose. Certainly it was necessary once in a while to change the pattern of things—she wasn't rigid. But her inability to propel herself down the aisle, then having her sleep taken over by some hot-blooded hunk who seemed to be trying to deliver some sort of warning she couldn't remember jarred every plan she'd made for her future.

And how totally insane did that all sound?

"He's all in your head," she muttered, dragging a hand through her long hair. She had other things to think about, she reminded herself. Although she'd been off duty for the past two weeks she had immersed herself in the details of a cold case homicide of a young woman in which a recently recovered automatic was the murder weapon. The Louisiana cop who'd found the weapon was due in her office this morning to transfer the automatic into her possession.

Even as that quiet assurance escaped her lips, an awareness vibrated in her nerves. And she knew, beyond all reason, all logic, that the man who swept her nightly into a dark storm of feelings did not come to her in a dream.

He was a memory.

Chapter 1

"Looks like Lizzie's running late this morning."

"When I called Sergeant Scott, she said she would meet me in her office." Sam Broussard scowled at the short, balding detective who'd led him to the closed door at one end of a murky basement corridor in the Oklahoma City P.D.'s headquarters building. "Eight o'clock sharp."

The cop who'd introduced himself as Kostka slid a key into the door's lock and swung it open, releasing a whiff of musty air into the hallway. The space beyond the door reminded Sam of a windowless black cave.

It matched his dark mood.

"When did Lizzie make that appointment with you?" Kostka asked while reaching in and flipping on the office's overhead lights.

"I called her from Shreveport two weeks ago today," Sam answered, wondering why the hell that mattered. "She said she was flying to Vegas that afternoon to get married, and would be back at work this morning."

Which was the start of the first leave time Sam had taken since the tragedy that had thrown his world out of whack. Time off his lieutenant had ordered him to take.

Kostka rubbed his double chin. "That'd explain it."

"Explain what?"

"Lizzie's experienced a few…personal complications lately." Kostka stuck a hitchhikerlike thumb toward the office. "Why don't you get settled while I give her a call?"

Sam remained in the dim corridor while his narrowed gaze took in the neat-as-a-pin desk in the cubbyhole-size office, its walls lined with battered black filing cabinets. He doubted Liz Scott's *personal complications* could get anywhere near to the damnable ones he'd endured. Even after two and a half years the guilt still ate at him like acid.

The one thing—the *only* thing—that had eased that searing ache was the intense edginess he felt a month ago when he recovered the .45 Colt.

The thought of the weapon that had been linked to one of Oklahoma City's cold case homicides had Sam peering around the office's door to see if he could spot a second desk. He didn't.

"Does Scott have a partner?" he asked.

"No," Kostka answered. "The OCPD received some

sort of grant to open the cold case office a couple of months ago. Got funding for only one detective position. That'd be Lizzie's."

Sam knew he could turn over the evidence envelope he had carried in from his SUV to the department's property room, then get back on the road to the vacation he had no desire to take. But leaving the Colt wouldn't help him figure out why the instant he'd touched it, he felt the equivalent of a rasp running right up his spine to the base of his skull.

Each day the gun had stayed in possession of the Shreveport P.D., that feeling had intensified. Which was something Sam hadn't shared even with his own partner, much less his Grandmother Broussard. One mention of his edgy unease, and the self-professed—and very superstitious—conjure woman who'd raised him would have mixed up one of her infamous herb bags of who-knew-what green leafy substances, with instructions for him to sleep with it under his pillow.

Even if he didn't give a damn about the case the Colt connected to, Sam knew all too well how defense attorneys could twist chain-of-custody issues to get evidence tossed out. Thirty years had passed since the automatic was used to murder a woman. With the case still unsolved—and a motherlode of evidence found *inside* the gun—he didn't want to risk having a judge rule the Colt inadmissible just because the cop who recovered it had failed to turn it over to the current officer of record on the case.

"I'm late! I'm sorry I'm late."

The harried female voice and hurried clip of footsteps on the dingy tile floor had Sam looking over his shoulder.

Despite the dim lighting, he could tell that the tall, long-legged woman rushing his way was a knockout. Her skin seemed flawless, her face a perfect oval. Her hair was slicked back and twisted into a braid that hung over one shoulder. As she moved, one flap of her turquoise jacket fanned back to reveal the gold badge and holstered automatic clipped to the waistband of her black slacks.

When she got close enough for him to see that her hair was flame-red, a feeling of familiarity hit him. But if they'd ever met before, he couldn't name the place or time.

"Welcome back, Lizzie," Kostka said. "I was about to settle your visitor in your office and give you a call."

"Thanks, Kostka, I owe you."

"And don't forget it." Behind the older man's grin, Sam saw the sharp assessment in his eyes as he gave her a quick going over. "I heard about the latest…glitch in your plans. You okay?"

"Fine. I'm fine."

It took Sam by surprise to find himself fighting the impulse to reach out, trail his fingertips down the knotted cable of her hair to find out if it felt as fiery as it looked. Instead he offered his hand. "Sergeant Scott, I'm Detective Broussard, Shreveport P.D."

"Detective," she said, extending her hand. "Sorry I wasn't here when you arrived."

The instant her palm pressed against his, Sam felt heat zigzag between them like a bolt of lightning.

"You're here now," he said, and suspected she'd felt the sensation, too. Why else would her eyes narrow, or her hand linger in his a moment longer than necessary?

"Guess I'm done here," Kostka said, turning toward Sam. "Pleasure to meet you, Broussard."

Sam returned the detective's handshake. "Thanks for the escort."

"No problem," Kostka said, then ambled down the hallway toward the elevator.

"I planned to arrive early and have things organized for when you got here," Liz said across her shoulder as she stepped into her office. She plopped her black leather tote bag on the desk, then turned back to face him.

Beneath the office lights, Sam saw that her eyes were ice-green. A tingle touched the back of his neck like a cool wind. Again, he felt a sense of familiarity, as though he'd gazed into those green eyes before, but had no memory of where or when. All he knew for sure was that if his grandmother ever got wind of this, she'd get her sister and cousins together for a mass tarot card reading.

"Then…." Liz lifted a hand, let it drop. "Time just got away from me."

Stayed home for a quickie with the new husband? Sam wondered. She wasn't wearing a wedding ring, but neither had he. There were plenty of ways for do-wrongs to get revenge against a cop. No sense telegraphing that the cop had a spouse someone could go after.

Sam settled in the sole chair at the front of the desk that Scott had waved him toward. He noted her office was ruthlessly organized. File drawers were neatly closed, papers stacked, their edges aligned.

Some instinct told him she ran her life that same way. "So, what do I call you now?"

Her copper-colored brows drew together. "Now?"

"When we talked on the phone, you said you were flying to Vegas to get married. You going by your husband's last name?"

"Oh." She looked away toward one of the window-less walls, but not before Sam saw the color rise in her cheeks.

Great, Liz thought. Well, she had to deal with her acquaintances and coworkers being privy to the mor-tifying details of how her personal life had imploded, but she did not have to share them with a total stranger like Broussard.

And she didn't care for the shock that had run up her arm when his hand had closed around hers.

"I'm still going by Scott," she said vaguely and studied him out of the corner of one eye while tugging a thick legal-size envelope out of her tote bag.

Broussard was tall, lean and broad-shouldered, dressed in black chinos and a charcoal canvas shirt with its sleeves rolled up on his forearms. Even though it was mid-fall, his skin was deeply tanned, his dark, shaggy hair shot with gold highlights from the sun. A rough shadow of beard darkened his cheeks and jaw. His features were chiseled, more rugged than refined, giving him the all-American jock look a lot of cops had.

"I remember you saying you'd be stopping here on your way to Colorado," Liz said while stowing her tote in the bottom drawer of her desk. "So we can deal with the transfer of evidence paperwork first thing and get you back on the road."

He glanced down at the envelope in his left hand, then lifted his gaze back to hers. Something flicked in his eyes, then disappeared before she could read it. "I'm not in that much of a hurry."

His voice had a killer rough-sweet quality, gravelly and totally sexy, with a noticeable Louisiana accent. The way her heart rate hitched at the slow drawl had Liz locking her jaw. With a real-life ex-fiancé and a dreamed-up hunk lover, the last thing she needed was to get the hots for some Louisiana cop just passing through.

Caffeine, she thought. Strong, cop coffee was what she needed to get her system leveled.

"Since you've got spare time," she said, "how about I go down the hall and pour us some coffee?"

"Sounds good."

In the five minutes it took her to retrieve the coffee and settle behind her desk, Liz had regained her composure. She had reminded herself that showing up late for the first time in her law enforcement career was not a capital offense. What mattered in the big scheme of things was that she was back at work. Her mistake had been taking off the two weeks she'd planned to be on her honeymoon. Spending that time mostly alone hadn't done her nerves any good—didn't her recurring dream prove that? Once she slid back into the routine at work, she was sure her life would get back on track. Even though it wouldn't be the *married* life she'd envisioned for herself.

"Since you've been off, I guess you haven't had time to review the homicide file the Colt connects to," Broussard said before taking his first sip of coffee.

"Actually I have." She opened the thick envelope she'd pulled from her bag and tugged out its contents. "I took the file with me to Vegas."

One of his dark brows quirked. "I'd say working while on your honeymoon is beyond the call of duty."

Liz gave him a tight smile. "I'm dedicated." And way thankful she'd been able to immerse herself in the details of the thirty-year-old murder and forget her own heart-wrenching troubles for a time. "So, Detective, you said you recovered the Colt in a cellar at a farmhouse on the outskirts of Shreveport?"

"Busted a fencing operation there," Broussard said and frowned.

"Something wrong with your coffee?"

"No. Sergeant Scott, have we met before?"

Regarding Broussard from across her desk, Liz didn't realize the side-trip her mind had taken until she found herself comparing his eyes to Dream Lover's. The shape might be similar, but instead of a shocking blue color, Broussard's eyes were a hard gray that reminded her of rocks hacked out of a cliff.

And *he* was real, flesh and blood. A prime piece of eye-candy. She *definitely* would have remembered if they'd ever crossed paths.

"I'm certain we've never met, Detective. Why do you ask?"

"Because you look familiar. Very."

"I don't have a clue why," she answered.

He sipped his coffee, watching her over the rim of his cup. "Have you ever been to Shreveport? Maybe attended a law enforcement conference somewhere in Louisiana?"

"No, to both." Liz rubbed her forehead where a headache brewed. After two weeks of having her sleep interrupted each night, she had to struggle to keep her thoughts sharp. "Can we get back to the Colt?"

"Yeah." Leaning forward, Broussard handed the evidence envelope across the desk. "I put a copy of my report, our firearm examiner's and the lab's inside."

Liz slid open the envelope and pulled out a clear plastic baggie containing the blue steel automatic. *Wish you could talk,* she thought, gazing down at the weapon that had ended a woman's life decades ago.

Setting the Colt aside, she slid the reports from the envelope. "Instead of my sitting here reading these, why don't you give me the highlights?"

"All right." Leaning back, Broussard rested an ankle over his knee. "It's hard to say how long the fencing operation we busted has been in business, but some of the stuff we found had been there a long time."

He inclined his head toward the desk. "Like the Colt. It was in the cellar in a plastic storage bin filled with guns.

"A lab tech ran all the weapons through NCIC. We got a hit that the Colt had been reported stolen thirty years ago in Oklahoma City. When our examiner tried to do a ballistics test fire, he discovered the Colt was jammed. He disassembled it and found the trace evidence I told you about on the underside of the slide."

"A small piece of latex, skin tissue and blood." The investigator in Liz couldn't suppress a smile. "You have to figure the latex is from a surgical glove worn by someone who shot the Colt. And that he placed his hand too high on the grip, then squeezed the trigger. The slide came back, then forward so fast, he probably didn't even know what 'bit' him."

Broussard nodded. "That shooter could be the person who killed your victim."

"If so, after thirty years we now have his or her DNA." Liz lifted a hand to finger the tail of her braid. "The timing on this is amazing."

"How so?"

"This office has been in existence only a few months, and I've been playing catch-up. It wasn't that long ago I submitted the ballistics information on the shell in that specific homicide to the ATF's database."

For the second time, Broussard regarded her over the rim of his cup. Beneath the office's bright lights, his smoky-gray eyes looked as hard as the strong lines of his beard-stubbled jaw.

"Then I recovered the weapon that fired that shell," he said. "Sounds like good timing on both our parts."

All at once, a gut-clenching uneasiness came over Liz. Despite his laconic Southern drawl, Broussard radiated an edgy, dangerous energy through every pore. Just like Dream Lover.

Her internal alarm system began blaring. Comparing every man she encountered to the one who'd taken over her dreams was not the most advantageous way to keep a grip on reality. Best to get Broussard out of her hair so she could immerse herself in work.

"If you'll walk to the property room with me, I'll sign the Colt into evidence and give you a receipt that confirms you transferred possession to me," she said. "Then you can get on with your vacation."

"Yeah." He tapped his fingertips against one arm of his chair. "First, though, I'd like to hear the details on the homicide the Colt links to."

Liz eased out a breath. She felt unnerved and antsy because her personal life was in such disarray. That was no reason to shove Broussard out of her office before he was ready to go. After all, if *she* had recovered evidence that linked to a homicide in another jurisdiction, she would instinctively want to know about the case.

Setting her coffee aside, she opened the file folder containing the details of the thirty-year-old murder. The reports inside smelled dry and dusty, slightly enhanced by something so subtle, Liz could only ascribe it to ancient memories.

"The victim was Geneviève Windsor." Liz retrieved a photo clipped inside the folder. The black-and-white picture showed a smiling, attractive young woman with long, wavy hair.

"A looker," Broussard commented when Liz handed him the photo. "Young."

"Twenty-three years old. She worked as an admin assistant to the CEO of an oil company. The day she died, she told a coworker a guy wouldn't leave her alone. Geneviève didn't say who he was, but the coworker assumed it was the marine Geneviève had been dating."

"His name?"

"Max Hogan. That night, Geneviève called police dispatch, begging for help. When a patrol cop arrived, her apartment was on fire, and she'd been shot and had fallen off the rusted fire escape behind her building."

"Did Hogan shoot her?"

"It was assumed he did, since his body was found near hers. He apparently was also on the fire escape, which collapsed under his weight. His neck was broken in the fall."

"What about the murder weapon? Did the detectives back then speculate why it wasn't found at the scene?"

Liz nodded. "There was an alley right behind the apartment building that was on the route from the downtown bus station to a homeless shelter. The detective's theory was that Hogan dropped the Colt when the fire escape collapsed. The gun landed in the alley and was scooped up by some homeless person before the cops secured the scene."

"What about the marine? When his body was found, was he wearing latex gloves?"

"No, and no gunpowder residue was found on either of his hands."

"There would have been if he'd fired a gun that night."

Liz nodded. "After you called me, I talked to the CSI in your lab who ran the DNA profile from the tissue found inside the Colt. The profile isn't complete yet, but the blood type doesn't match the marine's."

"So, there was a third person at the crime scene."

"The killer." Liz added the reports Broussard had given her to the folder.

"What's your game plan?" Broussard asked. "Who do you talk to first?"

Liz pursed her lips. Broussard wasn't acting like an off-duty cop, itching to start his vacation. "An interview with David York. He was an attorney thirty years ago when he reported the Colt stolen during a burglary of his residence."

"Any suspects in the burglary?"

"More than just a suspect. Patrol cops nabbed a guy who worked a deal for reduced jailtime by confessing to over one hundred burglaries. York's was one of them. Since his Colt wound up in your jurisdiction, I imagine you're going to want to take a close look at the burglar to see if you can link him to any old crimes in Shreveport."

Broussard nodded. "You're reading my mind. You said York *was* an attorney thirty years ago."

"He's a federal judge now. I have an appointment to see him this morning in his chambers." Liz checked her watch, saw it was nearly time to head to the courthouse. "So, Broussard, are you ready to go to the property room?"

"Sure," he said, but made no move to stand.

"Not to be inhospitable, but aren't you in a hurry to get on with your vacation?"

"No." He rose, his gaze locked on her face.

"No?" She didn't realize she'd been holding her breath until an odd wave of emotion tightened her chest. "Why not?"

"Your case has snagged my interest. And I'd much rather spend time sitting in on your interview with Judge York than get on with a vacation I have no interest in taking."

She studied him, trying to get his measure. "My session with York is just standard operating procedure. A cold case gets reopened, everyone involved has to be reinterviewed."

"I'm familiar with investigative procedures, Sergeant." He tossed his empty coffee cup into the wastebasket beside her desk, then turned back to face her. "You have a problem with my observing your interview?"

Liz refused to wither beneath his flinty stare. And her problem, she thought when the pulse in her throat started throbbing, seemed to be Broussard's effect on her hormones.

Wonderful.

"I don't have a problem, Detective," she said coolly. "You recovered the murder weapon, which makes you a principal in this case. You want to spend your free time working instead of relaxing, that's fine by me." She lifted a brow in subtle challenge. "Just remember who's in charge of this investigation."

One corner of his brooding mouth quirked, just a little. The smile, if that's what it was, didn't reach his eyes. "Something tells me if I did forget, you're more than capable of taking me down a notch."

"More than one," Liz countered, biting off the words. She grabbed her tote, annoyed that just the deep timbre of Broussard's voice made her feel as if she were plugged into a two-twenty line.

Chapter 2

Sam Broussard wasn't sure what the hell was going on. He could maybe write off his hinky feeling over the Colt to a cop's instinct, but that still didn't explain the sense of familiarity he'd felt the instant he saw Liz Scott.

Then there was the close-to-electric sensation he'd felt when they shook hands. Something was going on, and he was damn well going to figure out what it was.

So, here he sat at a hubcap-size table in the coffee shop at the Oklahoma City federal courthouse, waiting to observe the cold case cop's interview with a judge who'd gotten held up in a hearing that had run long.

Sam slid his gaze to Liz Scott, who sat beside him sipping coffee while she reviewed the details of the judge's thirty-year-old burglary report. She had some face, Sam reflected. No man could ever forget that flawless skin, the sculpted nose and direct green eyes.

Which was why he was positive now they had never met. So why had he been hit with the wave of recognition?

Maybe it was because he'd known other women who exuded the same sensuality she did. Other women who could pull a man in with a single look. Or he could be doing what he'd done since he was a boy— feeling certain he'd met someone before when doing so would have been impossible. His grandmother often declared that he experienced the hazy sense of familiarity because it was in his blood.

There'd been a time in his past that Sam had discounted his grandmother's herb bags, crystals and the spirit bottles she hung in trees, and just accepted her as the lovable eccentric who'd raised him after his parents died in a car wreck. That was before Tanya came along. Sam knew for the rest of his life he would feel a raw ache over the casual way he'd ignored his grandmother's portending of doom.

He tightened his grip on his coffee mug and shifted his dark thoughts to the woman sitting beside him. How the hell could she be *in his blood* when she'd gotten married two weeks ago? He had never poached on another man's woman and he wasn't about to start now. Still, he couldn't help imagining himself slowly sliding each pin from Liz's thick braid until that fiery mane tumbled down her back.

The thought put a knot in his chest. Tanya had had red hair, too, but not the same shade as Liz Scott's. He'd plunged his fingers through Tanya's hair uncountable times. Then, over the years, their marriage had gone to hell. He'd wound up hurt and angry and hadn't even wanted to touch her.

Then he'd as good as gotten her killed.

Since then, he'd worked relentlessly. His job was all he had, all he'd wanted. All he would ever allow himself to want.

At that instant, Liz lifted her gaze and looked him right in the eyes. Damn if he didn't feel a jolt go straight through him. He hadn't seen big, smoldering green eyes like that since—

Since he didn't know when.

"J. D. Temple hit the jackpot when he broke into York's home," Liz said. "In addition to the Colt, the loot stolen included a large coin collection, high-dollar jewelry, loose diamonds and numerous serving pieces of solid silver."

Sam squinted past her shoulder at the poor-quality microfilm copy of the burglary report. "York's law practice must have done pretty well back then."

"That, and he's an author. He's written several books on the English legal system, and is considered an expert on medieval law. He still lives in the same house he did thirty years ago, which is in the snooty part of town."

Her dry use of the term had Sam's mouth curving, even while his senses ran wild with her alluring scent.

She smelled good, like the flowers that bloomed in his grandmother's garden at night.

He didn't want to notice Liz's scent any more than he wanted to notice the slender arch of her throat. Or any of the other attributes he found impossible to ignore. Because he couldn't help himself, he drew an appreciative breath and felt the knockout punch of desire. *Don't go there,* he cautioned himself and forced his thoughts back to the three-decades-old burglary.

"Did any of Temple's other victims live in the snooty part of town?"

"The majority of the one hundred burglaries he confessed to were within five miles of the judge's house."

"So, Temple was a discerning thief." Sam sipped his coffee. "In the property we recovered at the bust in Shreveport, there were a lot of pieces of silver—coffee services, trays, vases. Also jewelry and coins. The judge's Colt wound up there. I wonder if there were other items from the burglaries Temple copped to."

"Highly possible. I'll be sure and ask him what fences he dealt with when I interview him at the state pen tomorrow."

Sam raised a brow. "Don't tell me he's still in slam for those thirty-year-old burglaries?"

"No, his lawyer worked a deal that got him ten years for those. Temple kept a low profile after his release until he broke into a house owned by a rich widow. After assaulting her, he charged out the back door where the woman's chauffeur tackled him and called the cops. That bought Temple a ticket back to the pen."

Sam watched while Liz aligned her notes, tapping the edges neatly together before returning them to a folder with WINDSOR printed on the tab in bold, precise letters. He wondered how all that controlled organization transferred into her personal life. And if her new husband found it as intriguing as he did.

"Sounds like you spent a lot of time while you were on leave digging through the background on this case."

With what looked like careful deliberation, she slid the folder into her tote. "Like I said, I'm dedicated."

"And your husband must be a real understanding guy for you to take work on your honeymoon. He a cop, too?"

"No." Her gaze stayed on his for a split second, then flicked away. "Look, I…When we got to Vegas we didn't…I just couldn't go through with it."

She looked back at him, and for the first time Sam realized she was wiped out. The fatigue was hard to spot, but it was there—in the sight drooping of her eyelids, the faint shadows under them.

Without conscious thought, he softened his voice. "You didn't get married?"

"No."

Sam felt his gut clench. The thought that she was no longer forbidden fruit was entirely too appealing. "Maybe you'll be able to piece things back together."

"No." The almost whispered word rang with finality.

He was aware that everything inside him was now at attention. "If you had doubts, calling off the wedding was the smart thing to do."

A line formed between her brows. "You an expert on marriage, Broussard?"

He hesitated, thrown off balance that he'd nearly told her he was a widower. He *never* talked about Tanya. Couldn't even think about her without seeing her lying in a pool of blood, and feeling the slicing guilt because he'd as good as put her there.

He set his jaw. Maybe he'd almost dropped his guard with Liz because of the fatigue and vulnerability he'd just seen in her face.

He didn't know. All he knew was he was going to have to keep a tight rein on his emotions.

"Broussard?"

Realizing Liz was waiting to find out if he considered himself an expert on marriage, he shrugged. "A common-sense observation, is all."

Just then, the cell phone she'd placed on the table trilled. Thirty seconds later, she ended the call, then dropped her phone into her tote and met Sam's gaze. "That was Judge York's secretary. He'll see us in his chambers now."

"Great." Sam could have sworn he felt Liz's gaze like a touch. So much for the tight rein on his emotions, he thought and rose.

For Liz, it was a relief to get out of the coffee shop. The entire time there, she struggled to stay focused on York's burglary report. More than once she'd lost her train of thought and found herself watching Broussard's hands. Noting how solid, strong and long-fingered they seemed.

And ringless.

What the heck was going on? she wondered as she and Broussard stepped onto an elevator where two maintenance men were debating the reasons why the heating system on the building's upper floors had gone wonky. While the elevator zoomed upward, Liz reminded herself that her thoughts should be centered on the Geneviève Windsor homicide. Instead she felt her senses being pulled—*tugged at*—by the gray-eyed Shreveport cop who planned to leave town as soon as this interview with the judge was over. Considering her overall brainless reaction to the man, that couldn't happen soon enough.

"After you," Broussard said when the elevator reached the courthouse's sixth floor.

"Thanks." Stepping past him into the overwarm corridor, Liz caught a whiff of his subtle woodsy cologne, and felt her pulse rate bump up. *Enough,* she told herself. She hadn't even felt this edgy, all-consuming pull to Andrew, and she'd almost married him. Twice.

The reminder of how her personal life had done a one-eighty had Liz's fingers tightening on the strap of her leather tote. Then there was the damn dream she'd had to contend with night after night that had left her weary beyond measure. She *had* to come up with a plan to get rid of her macho Dream Lover. Tonight.

Feeling marginally better, she tugged open the

heavy wooden door that displayed Judge David York's name.

Moments later, a middle-aged secretary escorted Liz and Sam into the judge's chambers. The large office, which was even warmer than the corridor, had the feel of an old-world study with dark paneled walls, leather chairs and a polished mahogany desk the size of a helipad.

The man sitting behind the desk was lanky, with sharp features and silver hair that lent him a distinguished air. From the background check she'd run, Liz knew that David York was in his mid-sixties, yet he looked a decade younger.

"Judge York, I'm Sergeant Scott, this is Detective Broussard," she said, flashing her badge as they moved toward the desk. Making the introductions automatically identified her as the lead detective. At this point, there was no reason to explain where Sam was from or why he was there.

"Have a seat." York gestured toward twin leather visitor chairs, his gold cuff link glittering with the movement. "The hearing this morning that pushed your appointment back has crimped my schedule. I have to be in court shortly, so I don't have a lot of time."

"I'll be brief, your honor," Liz said, settling into the chair beside Sam's. "The cold case office has reopened an unsolved murder in which the weapon used was a .45 automatic. A check of all unsolved shootings around the time of the homicide revealed that this particular murder was our only one in which a .45 was used."

The judge lifted one salt and pepper brow. "Perhaps because a .45 is an unusually large caliber weapon for street crime."

"It is," Liz agreed. "When we ran a check of all .45's reported stolen during the time frame of the murder, we got a hit on your residential burglary."

York blinked. "You're here about *my* burglary? From thirty years ago?"

"Yes." While working in Homicide, Liz had learned to always keep details close to the vest. Judge or no judge, York didn't have a need to know at this point that his Colt had been recovered, much less that it had been identified as a murder weapon. "More specifically, we're here about the man who confessed to breaking into your home and stealing your .45 Colt."

"I had my own law practice at that time," York said. "After he confessed, a police officer told me the man's name, wanting to know if I'd ever represented him. I hadn't." York remained silent for a moment, and Liz could almost see his mind working behind his dark brown eyes. "Apparently you're thinking that the burglar committed the murder? With my Colt?"

"It's possible," Liz said. "By his own admission, he stole the same caliber weapon used in a killing around the same time."

When she leaned to pull her copy of the burglary report from her tote bag, her gaze flicked to Broussard's right hand, resting on his thigh. In the next heartbeat, she imagined those long, tapered fingers pressing against her flesh. Her pulse began to thrum.

Liz swallowed hard, appalled she had allowed that type of thought to intrude while she was conducting an interview. Fatigue, she reasoned. Sleep deprivation had made her punchy.

Squaring her shoulders, she glanced down at the burglary report. "Judge, you told the officer your home was broken into while you were on vacation, so you couldn't be sure when during the week you were gone that the break-in occurred."

"That's correct."

"After this much time there's no way for me to know if all follow-up reports about your break-in wound up in the file, so I need to ask you a few questions."

York flipped a wrist. "Go ahead."

"Were you ever able to narrow down the time frame of when your house was broken into? Maybe learned something later from a neighbor who watched your property? Or your paperboy? Delivery people who might have routinely made calls in the area?"

"No, Sergeant. Unfortunately. However, it did occur to me later that the Colt might not have been stolen by the burglar."

Liz leaned forward in her chair. "Why?

"Not long before I went on vacation, I had some construction work done at my home. Part of that involved minor renovation to the kitchen. Numerous workmen were in and out, and it's possible one of them took the Colt before the burglary occurred."

Liz nodded. "Did you give the information about the

workmen to the burglary detective assigned to your case?"

"I phoned him," York answered. "He said he would make a note for the file."

"Do you remember the name of the construction company that did your renovation?"

"Sorry, no," York said. "It was a long time ago."

Nodding, Liz glanced at the report. "You didn't have a security system, right?"

"Correct." York gave her a rueful look. "I had one installed the day after I returned home and discovered the burglary."

When Liz noted the judge checking his watch, she said, "Just a couple more questions, your honor. The report states you purchased the Colt a few months before it was stolen."

"Yes."

"Did you fire it? Perhaps take it out for target practice?"

"No, I never shot the Colt." He pursed his mouth. "You look disappointed, Sergeant Scott."

"Just trying for a long shot, Judge." With the office so warm, she shoved up the sleeves on her jacket. "I was hoping you took your gun to a friend's acreage for practice shooting. And that the friend still owns the property."

She saw something akin to shock settle in the judge's eyes, then astonishment crossed his face. The look was replaced by uneasiness as his skin paled.

Liz exchanged a look with Broussard. He seemed as baffled as she by York's reaction.

She eased forward. "Your honor, is something wrong?"

"No." He rubbed a hand across his jaw. "I just… It's the heat in here." His eyes narrowed on her face. "Ballistics," he said after a moment. "You were hoping I had fired the Colt so you could go to the property and try to retrieve cartridges it ejected. Then compare them with the bullet that killed the victim in your reopened homicide. Sergeant Scott, do you honestly think the cartridges would still be there after thirty years?"

"Odds are against it. But stranger things have happened."

"Yes," York agreed. "Time doesn't destroy everything." He leaned back in his chair, regarding her. "I'm impressed, Sergeant. Very."

The way his gaze had locked on her sent an uneasy sensation whispering through Liz. "I'm just doing my job."

"A job you've had a very short time."

She kept her expression neutral. She had never met York, had never testified in any trial he'd presided over. Had he checked up on her after she called and scheduled the appointment with his secretary? If so, why?

"That's right," she answered. "The cold case office has only been open a couple of months."

"Since I was instrumental in obtaining the federal grant to fund the office, I'm very aware of that." He steepled his fingers beneath his chin. "In fact, I had been told your name when you requested a transfer from Homicide to work cold cases. I intended to arrange to meet you soon."

And here she was, feeding him a certain amount of disinformation by purposely failing to mention his Colt had been recovered when her current assignment probably depended on staying in his good graces. "I'm a little low on the food chain to be aware of departmental politics, so I didn't know you had anything to do with that."

York shifted his gaze to Sam. "There is only one position in the cold case office. What is your connection to this investigation, Detective Broussard?"

Liz held her breath while tension knotted her belly. Had she made a mistake letting Broussard sit in on this interview? If he told York he'd recovered the Colt, the judge would instantly know she hadn't been totally candid with him. Considering York's connection to the cold case office, she could be looking at a transfer to the department's Information Desk.

"I'm with the Shreveport P.D.," Broussard said. Although the rich, Southern cadence of his voice was casual, Liz caught an adversarial glint in his eyes.

"I got a tip that the man who confessed to yours and the ninety-nine other burglaries here may have spent some time in Louisiana years ago," Broussard continued. "When I learned that Sergeant Scott was trying to connect him to an unsolved homicide, I touched base with her. We've got some old crimes in Shreveport that we'd like to clear, if possible."

A wave of relief rolled over Liz. She owed Broussard big-time for not tripping her up with the judge.

"I see." York rechecked his watch. "I'm due in court. Sergeant Scott, have I given you the information you need?"

"One last question," she said as she and Broussard rose in unison. Again, she was aware of his height, of his tanned forearms sculpted by hard muscle, his dark hair that a rake of one of his wide-palmed hands had disordered.

"Your question?" York asked when she hesitated.

Liz tore her thoughts from Broussard and noted the annoyance marring the judge's smooth features. Great, her scattered thinking was close to putting her in York's bad graces.

"You submitted a form listing all property taken from your home," she said. "Did you discover anything else missing later? Maybe some inconsequential property you didn't bother reporting?"

"No, the information on the initial form is complete. My insurance company reimbursed me for my losses long ago."

York rose and moved around the desk with the ease of a man with total confidence. Probably didn't hurt that he raked in big bucks from the books on English medieval law he wrote, Liz thought, taking in the polished tips of his black shoes and the tailored cut of his single-breasted dark suit.

"A pleasure to meet you, Sergeant Scott," York said,

offering her his hand. "I'd like to drop by your office and see just what the grant has enabled the OCPD to do."

"Sure." There was almost something possessive in York's handshake that forced her to hold back a shiver. "Just let me know when you can fit a visit into your schedule."

By the time Sam walked onto the sidewalk outside the federal courthouse, energy was shooting through him. He had no explanation for the instant, intense dislike he'd felt for York. Or the sudden protective instinct that had dropped over him like a net. But he instinctively knew *who* he was supposed to defend.

Liz Scott.

He paused beside her, his jaw tight. Why would *she* need protecting? At present, he was off duty and unarmed; the cold case cop had a .357 automatic holstered at her waist. If anything went down, she'd probably be doing the majority of the defending.

"That's one strange reaction," she said.

Wondering if she had somehow sensed what was going on inside him, Sam shifted to face her. When he saw her narrow-eyed gaze was focused on the courthouse instead of him, he used the time to examine her.

It was a beautiful October day, warm and smelling of fall and in the bright sunlight her hair was ablaze. For the second time that day, he had the quick image of his hands unplaiting that thick braid, of his fingers plunging into those long tresses....

Wishful thinking, he told himself and scrubbed a palm across his stubbled jaw. "What reaction?"

"York's." She met Sam's gaze, her green eyes filled with speculation. "I ask him if he took the Colt out to target practice thirty years ago and he looks like I hit him. Then he turns pale. Can't help but wonder what that was about."

"I'm wondering, too." And not just about York's odd reaction, but his own, Sam added silently. There were too many things linked to the Windsor murder investigation niggling at him, bugging him, things he couldn't logic out. What *was* it about this case? And the woman assigned to investigate it? Both seemed to have reached out and grabbed him by the throat.

Liz hitched the strap of her tote higher on her shoulder. "I don't imagine we'll figure out what's going on with the judge by standing around here."

"Agreed," Sam said and fell into step with her.

"Speaking of York, I appreciate you not messing me up with him," she said while slipping on her sunglasses. "Especially now that I know he pulled the strings to get the grant that funds my present position."

Sam shrugged as they reached her unmarked cruiser parked in one of the cop slots on the side of the courthouse. "Like with any investigation, the less information that gets out, the better."

"Amen to that."

While he fastened his seat belt, Sam watched Liz dig a key ring with two keys out of the console and drop it into the pocket of her turquoise jacket. "What's next on your agenda?"

"Dropping you off at your car." She checked for traffic before pulling out of the lot. "Then I'm taking a look at the building Geneviève Windsor lived in."

"The fire the night of the murder didn't burn down the place?"

"The building's mainly brick and the hose jockeys got there fast, so the damage was mostly confined to Geneviève's apartment. Over time, the place traded hands, then was boarded up for over a decade. A developer named Lassiter has started renovations. He lent me the keys so I can get in."

"The building's close by?"

"A couple of blocks."

"I'll ride along if you don't mind," Sam said, and caught the look she shot him while they cruised through an amber light.

"For a man who's supposed to be headed to Colorado for vacation, you don't seem like you're in a hurry to get there."

What Sam was in a hurry to do was find some answers. For two and a half years he'd immersed himself in his job, working nonstop while guilt and bitterness ate a ragged hole in his gut. He'd gone through the motions of a cop, believing there was nothing left of himself to put into the cases he worked.

Then he recovered the .45 Colt and felt a spark, the echo of the fire-in-his-belly he hadn't felt about the job in years. And believed was lost to him forever.

Now, he felt an almost urgent need to find out every detail about the case the Colt was connected to. And the investigator in charge.

Out of the corner of his eye, he studied Liz's profile, both angular and soft. He had no explanation for why his system churned with the inexplicable need to protect her. All he knew was he wasn't going anywhere until he found out why.

"Let's just say I'm more curious about your murder investigation than in a hurry to get to Colorado," he said.

"Suit yourself."

"I usually do."

Liz flexed her fingers against the steering wheel. In the car's close confines she was aware—too damn aware—of the heat from Broussard's body, of his nearness, of his scent seeping into her lungs. Why wouldn't the man just leave? Already she could feel her energy flagging from all the hours of sleep she'd missed over the past two weeks, thanks to Dream Lover. The last thing she felt prepared to deal with was her libido's off-the-chart reaction to a man who at times seemed remote to the point of being cold. Which, perversely, made her wonder what it would take to warm him up.

At least he didn't see the need to make idle chitchat while she wove through the heavy downtown traffic. Instead he used the time to call his partner. The call obviously went to voice mail, and Liz listened while he relayed the information about J. D. Temple. Broussard ended the call after asking his partner to run local checks on the convicted burglar, then get back to him.

Seconds later, Liz whipped the car into a space across the street from a four-story brick building. A skeleton of scaffolding had been erected spanning its entire front. Two men were on the scaffolding, installing a pane of glass in one of the upper window frames.

"When you told me the building was on the direct route between the bus station and a homeless shelter, I envisioned some sort of hovel," Broussard said. "This place looks good."

"Thirty years ago this area was leaning toward shabby," Liz said before opening the driver's door. When she rounded the hood to where Broussard waited, she added, "There's a revitalization of the entire downtown going on now."

Inside the building, the air carried the scent of fresh paint with a trace of sawdust.

"Lassiter said all of the interior work is done except for carpet installation," Liz said as she bypassed the elevator and headed for the stairs.

"What floor did Geneviève live on?" Sam asked, keeping pace on the staircase beside her.

"Fourth."

"You have something against using that elevator?"

"Just want to get some exercise." And avoid putting herself in as many small, potentially intimate settings with him as possible. Sliding him a look, she anchored her sunglasses on top of her head. "Having a problem keeping up, Broussard?"

"I'll let you know if I do, Scott."

At the top of the staircase they both paused. There was a closed door on each side of the landing.

"Which apartment was Windsor's?" Sam asked.

"On the left." Turning, Liz pulled the key ring out of her pocket and approached the door to the apartment where Geneviève Windsor had lived and died.

With each step, Liz felt the air around her turn hotter. Staler. The scent of sawdust and fresh paint was replaced with the smell of mold, dust and years of cigarette smoke and sweat.

"Broussard, do you…smell something?" Even to her own ears, her voice sounded far away.

"Fresh paint." He gave her a swift glance. "Are you okay? You look a little pale."

"Yeah…I'm fine." The strange odor grew heavier, suffocating. She felt sweat sheen her forehead.

Taking tiny breaths through her mouth to try to lessen the cloying smell, Liz jabbed the key in the dead bolt and grasped the doorknob.

Instantly heat seared her palm. Pain shot up her arm as she jerked her hand away. Her tote bag slid off her shoulder and landed with a plop on the floor.

"I can't…" She swayed suddenly, surprising them both.

"Steady." Sam clamped his hands on her shoulders. She'd gone deathly pale, and beneath his palms he felt as limp as if every bone in her body had melted.

"I'm…fine." Liz made a weak attempt to pull from his grasp, only to wobble against him.

"Whoa." Sam steadied her. "You look a long way from fine."

"Air. Just need…fresh air." Head spinning, she jerked from his grip, intent on heading for the stairs.

Her knees began to buckle. She stumbled sideways against the wall.

"Hey!" Sam caught her upper arms as she swayed.

"I'm fine." She struggled to pull back from him. "Fine."

His mouth was set in a grim line, his eyes sharp with concern. The realization swirled in Liz's brain that he'd gazed down at her with the same fierce look once before. But that was impossible.

"You damn well don't look fine."

With that, Sam swept her into his arms and headed down the stairs.

Chapter 3

Layered beneath Sam's acute concern for Liz's well-being was the abrupt satisfaction he felt the instant he scooped her into his arms and headed down the apartment building's stairs. It was as if a puzzle piece had snapped into place.

"Put me down, Broussard. Dammit, put me down!"

"As soon as we get outside." He'd already passed the second-floor landing and was closing in on the ground floor.

"No." She was rigid in his hold, her breath coming in short pants. "Put me down. *Now!*"

When he reached the lobby, Sam paused and inched his head back to study her. Her green eyes were flashing and there was color in her face now. *Lots* of color, starting at her throat and rising to pool in her cheeks.

He understood this wasn't just a woman in his arms, but also a cop. The last thing someone wearing a badge wanted to show was weakness. He figured that, in Liz Scott's book, almost collapsing in front of him fell into that category.

Slowly he lowered her to her feet, but kept his hands locked on her upper arms. He felt the tension vibrating through her, humming like a harp string.

"I'm okay. I'm fine."

"Glad to hear it. Even so, it won't hurt to take it easy for a few minutes."

She hesitated as if testing the sturdiness of her legs, then lowered onto the bottom step. "I left my tote," she said, her gaze skittering upward. "And the keys to the apartment."

"I'll get them."

Liz gave an abrupt nod. Although she would have preferred to show Broussard she was capable of going back upstairs for her belongings, she felt physically weak, as well as emotionally battered. She was not only dealing with a racing heartbeat and vague nausea that churned in her stomach, she was mortified over having almost passed out in his presence.

"Mind if I take a look around what was Geneviève Windsor's apartment while I'm up there?" he asked.

Light-headed, Liz met his gaze, wondering if he sensed she needed a few minutes alone. But his expression was one she had seen on cops ever since she pinned on her badge—neutral, watchful. It was a face that gave away nothing of the man within. And no hint of his reaction to what had just happened.

"Look around if you want. Take your time."

Without another word, Broussard stepped past her and headed up the stairs.

What the hell had just happened? Liz propped her elbows on her knees, covered her face with her palms and waited for the trembling to pass. Bizarre, she thought. Totally bizarre.

The air that had seemed so hot now felt cool against her skin.

Spreading her fingers, she peered between them at the building's sparkling refurbished lobby. The paint and sawdust she now smelled were exactly what she *should* smell. Not stale air, cigarette smoke and sweat.

Holy hell! Dream Lover, now this. Had lack of sleep brought on what had just happened? Or was it the result of something else?

And what about that sudden radar blip where she was sure that sometime in the past she'd seen Broussard staring down at her with heated relentlessness? Her mind racing, Liz narrowed her eyes. Had he also experienced some sort of déjà vu moment in her office when he insisted she seemed familiar?

She was a big believer that there was always a reasonable explanation for the most inexplicable occurrences. Dream Lover had shaken that belief. Her whoo-hoo moment upstairs now had her thinking she should race to the nearest shrink for a full work-up.

Moments later she heard footsteps on the stairs, and dropped her hands while tension quivered through her. No doubt about it, Broussard *had* to think she was a wack job.

"Keys are inside." He placed her tote bag on the floor at her feet then sat next to her on the step. The tread was narrow enough that she had to angle toward the wall to keep their sides from pressing together.

"How you doing, Liz?"

Even though she was still shaky, hearing him say her first name in his honey-and-smoke Louisiana drawl thickened her pulse. Sitting this close to him had her blood simmering.

Great. Just what she needed.

"I'm fine." Ignoring the nagging heat, she leaned her weight against the wall. "Thanks for the lift, Broussard."

"My pleasure. And the name's Sam."

He regarded her with an intensity that made her want to squirm. "I doubt you consider having to haul a fellow police officer down four flights of stairs a pleasure." She hesitated, then added, "Sam."

The corner of his mouth lifted. "If you were my partner, who's built like a fullback, I'd have minded." He resettled his weight, his hipbone rubbing hers. That intimate touch made Liz think of hot, sweaty skin and tangled sheets.

And her early morning erotic dream. *No,* she instantly cautioned. *Don't go there.*

"Want to tell me what happened up there?" he asked.

"I'm not sure." She scrubbed her fingertips across her forehead. "I haven't slept well lately, which might be why I suddenly got light-headed. Why the air felt so hot."

"You asked me if I smelled something. What did you smell?"

"Cigarette smoke and sweat. The air seemed so stale, *so old,* I couldn't stand to take a deep breath. And when I touched the doorknob, I could have sworn it felt like someone had taken a torch to it. I should have blisters," she added, staring down at her unmarred palm. "Crazy. I know all this sounds crazy."

Sam leaned back against the step above them, stretching his legs out. "I live in a state where some residents practice voodoo. So, it takes a lot for me to label something 'crazy.'"

"You don't believe in that stuff, do you?"

"I'm not sure what all I believe in these days." He studied her for a long moment. "Can't say that about my grandmother, though."

"Your grandmother?" Liz prodded.

"My parents died in a car wreck when I was one, so she took me in to raise. She, my aunt and a couple of cousins call themselves conjure women. Among other things, they gather nettles in a churchyard and boil them down for a drink they swear will cure dropsy."

Liz stared at him. "Dropsy?"

"Yeah." His eyes stayed locked on hers. "I'll tell you all about my family sometime."

If he was leaving town, there wouldn't be a "sometime," Liz thought. From long habit, she unconsciously stroked her thumb over the birthmark on her inner right wrist while glancing across her shoulder up the staircase. She intended to check out the apartment for herself, but she didn't want to tempt a replay of going weak while Broussard was around. "I'll try this visit again some other time."

His eyes took her measure. "So, you haven't been sleeping well. What about eating?"

"What about it?"

"You skipped breakfast this morning. When's the last time you ate?"

"What makes you think I didn't eat breakfast?"

"I'm a highly skilled gatherer of information." He shrugged when she rolled her eyes. "You were late for our appointment, so I doubt you took time to eat."

"Okay, Sherlock, your reasoning's sound. My most recent meal was dinner last night."

He checked his watch, then rose. "It's nearly noon. How about we grab lunch?"

She regarded the hand he offered before sliding her palm into his. "I take it you'll leave for Colorado after we eat?"

"No." He helped her to her feet. "Two reasons. One, I've got a twelve-hour drive facing me, and half the day's gone."

She was on the verge of asking what his second reason was when she realized he hadn't released her hand. His felt exactly the way it looked, hard and strong. Like his face, his eyes.

And her pulse had doubled at the contact.

"Also," he continued while she tugged her hand from his, "while I was upstairs, my partner called. Shreveport P.D.'s computers are down right now so he can't run J. D. Temple's name. No sense in me leaving here until I find out if your confessed burglar who stole the Colt from the judge was ever in the Shreveport area. If he was, I'm going to need a list of all the property taken from the burglaries here so we can compare that to what we recovered from the fencing operation."

"You can get copies of those thirty-year-old burglary reports *if* they can be found in the Bermuda Triangle of storage."

Because the electricity she'd felt when she and Sam first shook hands that morning was again shooting up her arm, Liz jammed her hand into her jacket's pocket. Unless he was blind, he would see that their contact left her frazzled. Oh, man. This was not good.

"Bottom line is, I need to book a room somewhere. Can you recommend a place?"

"There's a small inn on one side of Reunion Square."

"Reunion Square?"

"It's the downtown neighborhood where I live. The square is only a couple of miles from the cop shop. We can stop by there after lunch and you can check in."

When he didn't respond, she realized he was measuring her with a gaze so blatantly masculine, she felt her skin heat. Even as she fought against it, every hormone in her body went on alert.

"Is there something else?" she asked.

"I was just thinking about that Colt. How my recovering it might turn into something neither of us could have anticipated."

"You could be right," Liz agreed. She certainly hadn't expected to meet a man this morning who radiated so much innate, primitive sex appeal. So much that her body instinctively drew toward him instead of away.

Just like with Dream Lover.

It was solely because she was on edge, Liz told herself. Her reaction to Broussard was an echo of the tension she'd lived with for two weeks.

She moved aside to gather up her tote. When she turned back, she watched Broussard's gaze slip down to linger on her mouth. Her stomach muscles clenched as desire flickered inside her. *That,* she knew, was no echo.

She sent up silent thanks that Detective Sam Broussard would be gone in the morning.

"You're kidding, right?" Sam's partner asked that night. "You're not really staying in Oklahoma City, are you?"

"I am." Dressed in sweatpants and a gray Shreveport P.D. sweatshirt, Sam switched his cell phone to his other ear while he carried his shaving kit into the bathroom of his room in the small, cozy inn.

"Sammy, we must have a bad connection," Frank Ozmun commented, his voice resonating with its usual nicotine huskiness. "'Cuz you sound okay about being stuck there. Me, I'd be hacked I wasn't already at my family's cabin enjoying all that crisp mountain air."

"Call me dedicated." Sam stepped back into the room where antique furniture glowed in the soft lighting of lamps turned low. He hoisted his duffel bag onto a small love seat and dug out his running shoes.

"Doesn't sound dedicated to me. And do I need to remind you our lieutenant *ordered* you to take leave time?"

His partner's pointed reference to the turmoil Sam had gone through over the past two and a half years—hell, try *four* years—had his shoulders going stiff. He walked to the window that overlooked Reunion Square and shoved back one side of the drapes. Although the night was pitch-black, enough carriage lamps dotted the square that every storefront was illuminated in a pale yellow glow.

While he stared into the night, he felt the guilt and bitterness simmering inside him, leaving a foul taste he'd almost grown used to.

"I *am* on leave, Frank."

"Doesn't seem that way to me, son, what with your calling and having me run a burglar's name."

"And from that run, we now know that, thirty years ago, J. D. Temple got pulled over for littering in Shreveport a couple of miles from where we busted the fencing operation. One piece of property Temple stole in Oklahoma City wound up with that fence."

"The Colt," Frank said.

"The Colt," Sam echoed. "I need to get copies of all burglaries Temple confessed to so we can try to match more of the property we recovered to burglaries here."

"Minor detail, but those break-ins occurred three decades ago."

"True. But since we know for sure he was in our city, and he's now a suspect in a murder here, we need to look at Temple hard in relation to some of Shreveport's unsolved crimes. The OCPD cold case cop I'm working with has an appointment to interview Temple tomorrow at the state pen. I'm going to see if I can tag along so I can question him about what he was up to while in our jurisdiction."

"I'm not disagreeing that we need to talk to Temple. But like you said, he's locked in the state pen, so there's no rush to get more charges filed on him. If you were me, you'd postpone that interview. Tell the cold case cop you're on vacation and to mail copies of the burglary reports to you."

"I'm staying here," Sam said while he continued staring out at Reunion Square.

"And no amount of talking on my part is going to get you headed toward Colorado, right?"

"I got orders to take leave, Frank, so I did. It's my choice where I go. And what I do."

"Yeah," Frank agreed with resignation. "Well, give me a heads-up if you find out anything interesting when you interview the burglar."

"Will do."

After ending the call, Sam shoved the drapes back

wider, his gaze settling on the ten-story high-rise on the opposite side of the square. Liz Scott had mentioned she owned a loft on the top floor of the building known as The Montgomery. Sam lifted his gaze.

Was it her loft where lights glowed with a welcoming warmth against the cool autumn night? Was she there, maybe staring out into the dark, just like he was?

His eyes narrowed while memories stored in the vault in his mind stirred. For the first time in years he thought of the dreams he'd had while growing up. Dreams of a young girl with red hair. They'd been friends, played childhood games.

Was that it? he wondered. Did Liz Scott seem so familiar because she conjured up memories of those long-ago dreams? Dreams that changed as he grew. Dreams he abandoned when his feelings and needs for his friend became not so innocent.

His thoughts went to that morning after he'd carried Liz down the staircase of the refurbished apartment building. Sitting beside her on the staircase, he'd been consumed by emotion that was far from innocent. The lust that had hit him had been instantaneous, overwhelming and dangerous as hell. He'd wanted to absorb her distinctive scent, learn her textures. He'd hungered to taste her mouth, and run his hands over her skin.

It was the same kind of chemistry that had slammed into him years ago the instant he'd seen a long-legged redhead standing on the side of the road, glaring at the flat tire on her pickup. That chemistry had eventually led to disaster. Just because he apparently had a thing for redheads, Sam wasn't about to go there again with Liz Scott, no matter the need churning inside him.

He shoved the drapes closed then pulled on his running shoes. He left the hotel and jogged across Reunion Square, knowing even as his feet pounded the brick sidewalk, that a man could never outrun his past.

She *would* outwit Dream Lover.

With a mug of strong-enough-to-smelt-lead coffee on the nightstand, Liz sat in bed, a bank of pillows propped behind her. It was ten minutes to two in the morning. Outside the windows, the moon skimmed in and out of fat gray clouds, sending darting, silver images through her dark bedroom.

Although she'd gone off duty hours ago, she was conducting the equivalent of a stakeout. One that would result in her taking back control of her life.

Her gaze focused out the nearest window and across Reunion Square where a fan of soft light illuminated the inn's sign. Okay, so tonight she would take back control of a *part* of her life, she conceded.

She apparently couldn't do anything about the fact that just being in close proximity to Sam Broussard made her pulse throb through her veins like a freight train. It was the same type of reaction she might have to a lover.

Which Broussard definitely wasn't. And since she was still unsteady from her two recent couldn't-bring-herself-to-walk-down-the-aisle fiascoes with her ex-fiancé, getting up close and personal with another man was the last thing Liz intended to do.

And whatever it was in her brain that had conjured up Dream Lover needed to get that message. Which was why she was propped up in bed in stakeout-mode at the time Dream Lover always appeared.

She was wide-awake, so she couldn't have the dream.

Just as the first of two chimes from the clock in the old tower in Reunion Square sounded, a wave of weariness swamped her. Blinking, she glanced toward the nightstand to check her clock's luminous dial to make sure it was in sync with the square's. It was.

Suddenly the digital numbers blurred as exhaustion overwhelmed her. Helplessly she felt herself being pulled down into sleep.

She sensed his presence at the same instant the air against her flesh heated. Air that seemed to swirl, as if electrified with his anger over her attempt to evade him.

As always, his features were hidden in shadow. Only his eyes burned hot blue in the moonlight when he leaned over her.

"Sae wit be wel bewared! Touche not wat se cyning woulde enfeffe."

His voice rasped with fury across her bare flesh, his words foreign. Then his hands were on her and he was between her thighs, holding them wide so she had no control, no protection. He took her with a seething furious intensity while his blue eyes gleamed hot, showing her no mercy.

Nor, dammit, did she want any. Despite her best intentions, she found she wanted only the fierce intimacy of his hard body locked into hers.

He repeated the words, his voice, more urgent than angry now as passion replaced the fury she'd glimpsed in his eyes.

And then the moonlight dimmed. The air frosted. Shivers of dread engulfed Liz as a different pair of eyes filled her vision. Eyes that watched her with a feral intensity.

Waiting for her.

Wanting her.

"So, dream stud got ticked off because you were awake at the time he always shows up?" Allie Fielding asked Liz the following morning at the Paradise Bakery in Reunion Square.

"Yes." Liz anchored her forearms on the table tucked into one of the bakery's cozy corners. Outside the small bay window the sky was steel-gray, the clouds whipped by a crisp October wind. Indoors, the aroma of delicacies fresh from the oven scented the warm air.

"Hot sex with a hot stud." Leaning back in her chair, Allie used a manicured hand to fan herself. "You, girlfriend, are living every woman's fantasy." In the habit of changing her appearance daily, the owner of the square's sensuous lingerie shop currently wore her long blond hair Veronica Lake style. Her wide-set blue eyes were shadowed with a muted coral shade that matched her tailored business suit. As did the pink diamond studs that glittered at her earlobes.

"I'd give up that fantasy for one night of uninterrupted sleep," Liz said.

Allie's expression turned to concern. "What about seeing your doctor? He could give you something to help you sleep."

"Maybe," Liz said. Problem was, she figured sleeping pills would only block the dream for as long as she took the meds. What she wanted was to end it permanently.

"What about what Dream Lover keeps repeating to you?" Claire Castle settled a china plate holding three blueberry muffins the size of hubcaps in the table's center, then slid onto the chair between Allie and Liz. "Have you been able to remember any of what he's saying?"

"Bewared. And something that sounds like toosh or tush." Liz blinked. "This is the first time I've been able to remember any of what he keeps telling me."

"Bewared and tush," Allie repeated. "Anybody have a clue what that means?"

"It would help to know what language he's speaking," Claire said.

Sipping her latte, Liz saw the bewildered look that passed between her two closest friends. "I know all this sounds crazy. I'm crazy."

"No, you're not." Claire shook her dark hair back over the shoulders of the crisp white blouse she'd paired with a slim black skirt. "Think of what you've been through lately. All that stress and heartache would be enough to give anyone nightmares."

"Claire's right," Allie said while pinching off a bite of the muffin she'd snagged off the plate. "And think about this—your dream stud showed up the night you broke up with Andrew. Maybe that's because your subconscious knew you were supposed to be on your honeymoon, having glorious sex? So that's what you dreamed you were doing."

Liz felt something loosen inside her. One of the best things about having close girlfriends was knowing you could count on their support. Never once had either Claire or Allie shown one ounce of doubt that Liz wasn't actually experiencing the erotic dream. They just took her word for it.

Liz considered it a stroke of luck the night she'd stumbled over Claire and Allie outside their shops in Reunion Square, drinking champagne toasts to single life. The toasts included the ceremonial burning of a photo of Claire's ex-lover, a sexy federal agent. Instead of hauling the tipsy pair to jail, Liz had listened to Claire's tale of love gone bad, then joined in the photo burning, thus forging a steadfast friendship.

Claire was now happily married to the sexy fed. And Liz had finally gained the family she could only dream about during the years when foster parents had come and gone in a blur.

Knowing her friends were waiting for her to comment, Liz frowned while rubbing at the dull ache in her right temple. "But if my subconscious knew I was supposed to be on my honeymoon, shouldn't it be Andrew I'm having all that hot dream sex with?"

"No," Claire said firmly. "He wasn't the right man for you. Which is why you couldn't go through with either wedding."

Allie leaned in. "If you can just figure out *who* this hunk is, that might tell you *why* you're having this dream."

"Maybe." Having little appetite, Liz stared at her lone muffin still on the plate in the table's center while her thoughts focused on the previous day. Why, when she first met Sam Broussard, had she compared his eyes to Dream Lover's? She could understand doing that if their eyes were the same color, but slate-gray was a long way from electrifying blue.

"Liz?" Claire prodded. "Did you think of some other way to figure out who your dream lover represents?"

"No," she said, biting back frustration. "The guy in my dream doesn't exist. I *know* that. But there I was yesterday, comparing his eyes to this cop's who I'd just met. If that's not loony, I don't know what is."

Allie arched a perfect blond brow. "Were you wishing that cop was your studly hunk?"

Liz winced when she saw the look of interest her comment had put on her friend's face. Not even to her two closest friends would she admit that Broussard seemed to have the same blowtorch effect on her libido as Dream Lover.

"No, of course not," Liz answered. "The cop I met is with the Shreveport P.D. He just stopped by to drop off some evidence on his way to Colorado."

"My plans have changed."

Coming from just beside her, the deep voice with a touch of the South shimmering through it had Liz's spine going straight. Oh God, how much had Broussard overheard?

Slowly she lifted her gaze, and saw that he had his cop face in place, his eyes unreadable. When her gaze slid downward, she felt her mouth go dry. He was casually dressed in worn, nicely fitting—*really* nicely fitting—jeans and a gray sweater that matched his eyes and showed off an impressive chest and the muscles in his tanned arms.

She was a sensible, logical woman, but, Lord, he was *gorgeous,* and her own powerful, all-consuming reaction to the man shook Liz to the core. Yesterday at this time he'd been a stranger, yet in a mere twenty-four hours it was as if she knew him on some deep primitive level.

Which was just one more item to add to her growing list of weirdo things she'd experienced as of late.

"Are you going to introduce us?"

Allie's question jerked Liz's thoughts back to the present. "Of course. Allie Fielding, Claire Castle, meet Detective Sam Broussard."

"A pleasure, ladies," Sam said while he shook Allie's, then Claire's hand. "Liz told me she'd be here this morning, and if I dropped by she would treat me to coffee and the best muffin I'd ever tasted."

"She's right about the muffin," Allie said, giving him a smile. "So, you're headed to Colorado?"

"I was."

"Was?" Liz asked.

"Something's come up in the investigation. I need to talk to you."

"Allie, look at the time," Claire said and rose. "Neither of us will get our shops open if we don't hustle." She turned to Sam. "Sorry we can't stay and chat, but duty calls."

"Not a problem. Which business is yours?"

"Home Treasures, the antique shop two doors down. Drop in and browse if you have time before you leave Oklahoma City."

"I might do that. I have a grandmother who's fond of antiques."

Allie slid on her lush ebony cashmere coat while saying, "My shop is next door. If your grandmother has a yen for sexy lingerie, stop by Silk & Secrets."

Sam lifted a dark brow as he settled into the chair Claire had vacated. He waited until both women swept out of the bakery door, then looked at Liz. "Do grandmothers wear sexy lingerie?"

Beneath the bakery's bright lighting, his eyes looked like fathomless liquid silver. Liz glanced down at the table, trying not to notice. What was it about this guy that even his eye color drew her?

"According to Allie, women of all ages shop at her store."

"She'd better not count on *my* Grandmother Broussard showing up."

Liz smelled his subtle woodsy cologne, with undertones of soap from his morning shower. He gave her the unnerving feeling that he was crowding her space, but his chair was a foot from hers.

For heaven's sake, she needed to get a grip. *Now.* "What's come up?" she asked.

"I heard back from my partner last night." Sam pointed at the muffin still on the plate in the center of the table. "You going to eat that behemoth?"

"Help yourself." Hoping a few moments of distance would level her pulse rate, Liz pulled some bills out of the pocket of her hunter-green wool blazer. "You're here at my invitation so I'll grab you some coffee."

"Appreciate it."

His voice made her think of a slow-moving river. In direct contrast was the tension that vibrated inside her as she headed toward the bakery's counter.

Minutes later, she settled back at the table. "The investigation?" she prodded while Sam ate the muffin with enthusiasm.

"Like I said, I heard back from my partner last night. He got a hit when he ran J. D. Temple's name. Seems the convicted burglar got popped near the outskirts of Shreveport thirty years ago for littering."

Liz felt the investigator inside her stir. "Do you know the exact date?"

"One week after Judge York reported his burglary."

"Making it a few days after Geneviève Windsor's murder," Liz added.

Sam nodded. "I'm going to need that list of all the property taken in the burglaries Temple copped to. The more we can prove he sold to the fence we busted, the stronger your case in proving he had possession of the Colt that killed Windsor."

Just the thought of Sam staying in town had unease trickling through Liz. "You don't need to hang around here waiting for copies of those burglary reports. I can mail them to you."

He popped the last bite of the muffin into his mouth, then leaned back in his chair with his coffee. "You sound like my partner."

"How so?"

"He's been hounding me to go on vacation."

The edge that had crept into Sam's voice had her brows drawing together and she momentarily forgot about the tightness in her stomach. "Why has he had to hound you?"

Something moved in his eyes before a shutter came down. "Work has a way of keeping one's mind off of certain things."

Liz could vouch for that, having purposely immersed herself in the Windsor homicide case during the two weeks she'd planned to spend on her honeymoon.

"Is that why you're not in a hurry to head to Colorado?" she asked. "You'd rather work?"

Sam's gaze lingered on her face in a way that made the unsettled feeling in her stomach deepen. "If I take off now, I'll spend all my vacation wondering about some things."

Even as Liz felt heat rise in her face, she assured herself none of those things was her. "What things?"

"What J. D. Temple was up to thirty years ago while he was in Shreveport, for instance." Sam sipped his coffee. "The only hope I have of finding out is by talking to the man. You're going to the state pen to interview him, so if you let me hitch a ride there, I can talk to Temple, too."

"You're welcome to ride along," Liz said while shoving the end of her braid over one shoulder. From the edge she'd heard in his voice, she'd bet her paycheck there was a story behind why his partner thought he needed a vacation.

Although the female in her couldn't help but wonder if it had to do with a woman, she would never ask Sam about it. She would keep things on a professional footing—that was obviously the right thing to do.

She just had a sinking feeling that, considering the sexual energy crackling inside her like heated lightning, doing so might not be easy.

Chapter 4

In Sam's opinion, the thin, wiry man sitting in the Oklahoma State Prison's stuffy interrogation room looked more like a gray-haired grandfather than a hardened career criminal. What ruined the image was the washed out gray shirt with INMATE blazed in orange across the front and back, and the silver handcuffs circling J. D. Temple's wrists.

"You're a pretty good burglar, aren't you?" Liz asked from the chair beside Sam's. As she'd done the previous day with Judge York, Liz had taken the lead in the interview. The Windsor case was hers, and Sam was along for the ride. At least until he had a chance to find out what Temple had been up to thirty years ago in Shreveport.

"Yes, ma'am," Temple said genially. "B&E's how I made my living for a long time." He was in his sixties, serving twenty years for first-degree burglary and assault. Sam doubted Temple would ever be free again.

Liz nodded, her green eyes patient. Sam watched her, sitting beside him in her slim jade jacket, her mass of coppery hair trained back in some complicated braid that left her face softly framed. Heavy twists of gold glinted at her ears.

Yesterday, he had learned her interview technique was a lot like his. He knew instinctively that if he and Liz worked together for very long, they would be the type of partners who got their rhythm down as intimately as lovers. Which was the last thing he should be thinking about, considering the guilt-ridden hell his physical needs had gotten him into in the past.

"Detective Broussard and I are interested in one of the residential burglaries you confessed to pulling thirty years ago," Liz said.

"Yeah?" Temple lifted a gray eyebrow. "Which one?"

"This one." She pulled a digital photo of the judge's house out of the file folder on the table in front of her and slid it toward Temple. "Look familiar?"

"Sure does. That's on account I got this photographic memory." Temple's mouth curved with pride to reveal cigarette-stained teeth as he studied the picture. "While I cased this place, I took time to admire the fountain in the center of the curved driveway. Don't see a naked stone mermaid every day, you know."

"What else do you remember about the house?"

"That I left there with silver, jewelry and one hell of a coin collection. Had some mighty rare coins in it. I made a tidy sum off all that loot." Temple nudged the picture back toward Liz. "Especially the bracelet. All these years later, I sometimes still think about it. Wish I'd kept it, since I never ran across another one close to it."

"Which bracelet?" Liz voiced the same question Sam asked silently. On the drive to the prison, he'd studied the list of stolen property York had submitted after the burglary. It hadn't included a bracelet.

"The only one I took from the place. Gold with a red stone." Temple narrowed his eyes. "The band was a cuff, made of real gold and woven in some sort of knotted pattern. The stone in its center was something else. Had all these shades of red that seemed to swirl, like something inside it was alive and breathing. Hell, I could draw that bracelet for you if you want."

"We'll get to that," Liz said. "What did you do with the bracelet?"

"Sold it to a contact in Oklahoma City."

"What's his name?"

"Vic Dunn. He's been dead about twenty years, so it's not like I'm ratting him out by tellin' you his name. He ran a big fencing operation on the city's south side."

Liz tapped an index finger against the photo. "Three decades have passed since you broke into this house. Any chance you stole the bracelet with the red stone from some other place?"

"Nope. Like I said, I've got this great memory. Don't matter how much time has passed, I know where I got stuff and where I unloaded it."

"Then you ought to be able to tell us what you did with the .45 Colt."

Temple frowned. "What Colt?"

"The one you took from the same house where you stole the bracelet."

"I didn't take no Colt."

"The homeowner claims you did."

"Well, he's a lying dog." Indignation settled in Temple's voice. "I never took no gun from nobody. Ever."

"Not ever?" Liz asked. "You burglarized homes and businesses for decades. Do you really expect me to believe you never took guns from those places?"

"I can't do much about what you believe. All I can tell you is that when I was five, my big brother got shot in the head during a drive-by. He died, right in front of me. 'Cuz of that, I've never touched a gun. You can hook me up to a lie detector if you want."

Sam's gut-level reaction was that Temple was telling the truth. Still, the con had years of practice lying to cops and had maybe perfected the art.

"We may give you a polygraph at a later date," Liz said evenly as she pulled a second photo out of her folder. "How did you meet Geneviève Windsor?"

Temple squinted at the black and white photo Liz laid in front of him. "Don't know her."

"Are you sure?"

"Positive." He lifted his gaze. "I'd remember if I'd ever run across a pretty girl like that."

Liz returned the photo to her folder then looked at Sam. She was wearing her cop face, as emotionless as a mask, her green eyes shuttered so he couldn't tell if she was inclined to believe Temple. "Do you have questions, Detective Broussard?"

"Yeah." Keeping his expression benign, Sam leaned forward. "J.D., why don't you put that rock-solid memory to work and tell me what you were up to thirty years ago in Shreveport?"

Liz spent the initial half hour of the drive from the prison back to Oklahoma City on the phone, first briefing her boss, then talking to a chemist in the trace evidence lab. She'd just ended that call when Sam got through to his partner.

While she kept the unmarked cruiser at a steady pace along the interstate, Sam told his partner about J. D. Temple's claim that he hadn't boosted the Colt. Then Sam added, "He admitted he'd heard about a fence in Shreveport who paid top dollar. Temple said he had a trunk full of stolen loot when the cop stopped him for littering a quarter mile from the fencing operation.

"Claimed he got spooked and hauled ass back to Oklahoma City without seeing the fence. I told him since the statute of limitations on whatever crimes he pulled there expired long ago, I just needed him to tell me what all he'd been up to while in our jurisdiction so I could clear our books."

Liz slid Sam a look. He hadn't reminded Temple that any murders the con committed weren't covered under that umbrella. Which was exactly what she would have done. They'd read Temple his rights at the start of the interview. The con could have opted to shuffle back to his cell without saying a word. Instead, he *chose* to talk to them. She and Sam had been under no obligation to warn him not to implicate himself in any unresolved crimes.

The guardrails streamed by while Sam continued briefing his partner. Liz thought about the way he had leaned forward in his chair when she'd turned the questioning over to him. He hadn't encroached on Temple's space, just eased in enough to invite confidence, to suggest support rather than intimidation.

She had to admit she admired Broussard's easy interrogation technique. Then there was the spicy scent of his cologne, his rangy build, the snug fit of his jeans, the sharp contour of his rock-hard jaw, the steely-gray eyes. All of which presented a huge problem for her.

Considering the upheaval in her life right now, she should batten down the hatches when it came to the man sitting in her car's passenger seat. Especially since just listening to his smooth, rich baritone drawl added a bump to her heartbeat that she found both baffling and embarrassing.

"Okay," Sam said after ending his call. "Ready to go over what Temple told us?"

"Ready." Liz rolled her shoulders, determined to keep her focus off the man and solely on cop business. "Let's start with the Colt."

"All right. You've got a career burglar who admits to stealing tons of property, but swears he never took a gun from any of the places he burgled. Claims that's because his big brother died in a drive-by shooting."

"Which is a believable reason, if the story about the brother is true. That's on the top of my list of things to check out."

"For now, let's suppose it is true," Sam said. "Which would mean Temple didn't steal York's .45 Colt. So, maybe one of the construction guys who did work at York's house took it."

"It's possible." Liz bore down on the accelerator to pass an eighteen wheeler. "When I got back to the office yesterday afternoon I dug through the files. I couldn't find a note where York called the detective assigned to work his burglary to tell him that one of the workmen could have taken the Colt. Since York doesn't remember what company he hired to do the renovation, there's a chance I won't be able to find out who those workmen were."

"Might be impossible." Sam retrieved the file folder Liz had laid on the seat between them. "That's some bracelet," he said, pulling out the sketch Temple made before a guard escorted the con back to his cell.

Liz flicked a look sideways. "What were his exact words about the red stone? Its various shades seemed to swirl, like something inside it was alive?"

"And breathing," Sam added while he studied the sketch. "If Temple's recall is as good as he claims and he stole the bracelet from York's house, why didn't the judge list it on the stolen property form? If it was as valuable as Temple said, you have to figure York had an expensive bauble like that insured."

"He could have just forgotten to add it to the list of stolen items he submitted to the P.D. I'll check with the insurance company he had at the time and see if he claimed the bracelet with the other property."

Sam dropped the sketch back in the folder. "In regard to the fence in Shreveport, Temple swears he didn't do business with him. When I asked how property from a burglary Temple pulled in Oklahoma City wound up there, he said word was all over the street that the fence was paying top dollar for stolen goods. Mindful of his bottom line, Temple traded property from burglaries he pulled here to other do-wrongs who transported it to Shreveport."

"No way to prove or disprove that," Liz said.

"Not at this late date." Sam shifted, propping one shoulder against the passenger door. "So, Liz, why cold cases?"

"What?"

"Kostka, the detective who took me downstairs to your office yesterday, told me you worked Homicide for a few years, then requested a transfer when the department got the grant to open the cold case office. Why leave your prestigious assignment to Homicide?"

"It's hard to explain."

"Try."

"Okay." Liz eased out a breath while gathering her thoughts. "In school, my favorite subject was history."

The sun had finally penetrated the gray clouds, so she slid on her sunglasses. "I've always liked delving into the past and finding out what happened. My friend, Claire, looks at the antiques she acquires for her shop and tries to determine where they came from. What the people who owned them were like. What those people did. That's how I feel when I open a file on a crime that's never been solved. I want to know what the people involved were like. What they did. Why the bad things that happened to them happened. And I like how it feels when I'm able to give some of them closure they never had."

"Interesting."

Liz shrugged. "I know all that sounds strange."

"No, it doesn't," Sam said. "You're the equivalent of a cop anthropologist. Digging up the past and using new methods to solve old crimes. Nothing strange about that." His gaze stayed on her, and Liz felt the sharp assessment in his gray eyes. "As assignments go, working cold cases has risks."

"So does giving out parking tickets."

"Not the same thing. After a case goes cold, the bad guy relaxes, thinking he got away with it, that he buried his secrets deep enough. Years sometimes pass. Then you come along and start stirring up things. Puts you in a certain amount of danger."

"No more so than any other cop."

"Most cops have a partner. Or at least backup that can reach them in a few minutes."

Liz slanted him a look. "I can take care of myself."

"Didn't say you couldn't. It's just a good idea to have someone who adds a layer of protection."

When the exit sign for downtown came into view, Liz flipped the turn signal. Minutes later, she cruised into Reunion Square and braked at the curb in front of the inn where Sam had spent the previous night.

While the engine idled, she watched him unfasten his seat belt. "Are you going to wait until morning to leave for Colorado?"

"No."

"Well, then." The wrenching regret that hit her was unnerving. Hadn't she been wanting him to leave town since the moment he walked into her office? She forced a smile while offering her hand. "Nice doing business with you, Sam."

"Likewise." His fingers curved around hers, held firm. "What do you plan to do about what Temple told us?"

Liz glanced at their joined hands. She knew she should tug hers from his grasp, but didn't. His long, strong fingers were warm. His touch firm. Inviting.

"I'm going to wait until I hear back from the lab, which shouldn't be much longer," she answered. Thankfully the unsteadiness brought on by their flesh-to-flesh contact didn't sound in her voice. "If Temple's DNA profile on file at the prison matches the tissue from inside the Colt, I'll know he lied about stealing the gun."

"And if it doesn't match?" Sam asked while his thumb stroked over the birthmark on the inside of her wrist.

The action seemed to have too much influence over

her pulse. "Then I'll try to verify some of the other stuff Temple told us. If it all turns out to be true, I'll go back to Judge York and see if he can come up with the name of that construction company."

Sam's flinty gaze stayed locked on hers. "I'd like to act as backup on your investigation."

"Thanks, but I can handle things on my own."

"No doubt. I want to be in on it, is all."

"No one's saying you can't be. I'll keep you updated via e-mail."

"Not good enough." He shifted his gaze past her shoulder to stare out the driver's-side window. "Not where this case is concerned."

She studied his face in the late afternoon sunlight. His eyes couldn't seem to decide what color they should be, she thought. They were caught somewhere between gray and blue. *Dream Lover blue.*

Oh, hell.

She pulled her hand from his, curled her fingers into her palm. No way did this sexy cop from Shreveport have anything to do with Dream Lover. She was just tired. The demise of her engagement had been vicious, and to tumble from that into a recurring erotic dream would have shaken anyone. What she needed now was to get a handle on her emotions. She would have a lot more success at that as soon as Sam Broussard got on with his Colorado vacation.

She uncurled her fingers while easing out a breath. "I need to get back to my office. Like I said, I'll keep you fully informed on the investigation."

Sam kept his gaze on her, his eyes now a steely gray. It made her wonder if she'd just imagined them looking so blue. If maybe some part of her wanted him to be Dream Lover.

"There are some things about this case that have gotten under my skin," he said. "I want to stay here and see how this all plays out."

She thought about what he had said earlier about working cold cases. "Are you being mule-headed about this because you think I need backup? Some sort of protection?"

Sam skimmed his gaze down her long, trim figure, then up. An entire day had passed since they left Judge York's chambers and the sense that she needed protecting had dropped over him like a net. Overnight, the feeling had heightened. As had his fantasies about the hot, erotic things he was aching to do to her. With her.

He gave her a mirthless smile. "None of my reasons have anything to do with me being mule-headed."

"What about Colorado? Why stay here to investigate a thirty-year-old murder when you've got a chance to kick back and relax in all that cool mountain air?"

Sam knew the only way he would get clearance to work on an out-of-jurisdiction murder was if the cop assigned to the case requested his assistance. So, he was going to have to level with Liz about a few things. Just not everything.

"Going on vacation wasn't my idea. My lieutenant ordered me to take off. My partner's family owns a cabin in Colorado, which no one's using right now, so he loaned me the key. I figured it was as good a place as any to spend my forced leave time."

She narrowed her eyes. "Why did your lieutenant order you to take vacation?"

"He decided I'd been working too hard. Close to getting burned out."

"Were you?"

"It didn't feel like it, especially after I recovered the Colt."

"What if your lieutenant's right? If you're close to getting burned out, you need—"

"I'm not getting close," he countered. "And what I need is to stay here and work on this case with you. Maybe that'll help me figure out some things."

"What things?"

Sam felt his frustration level kick up a notch. Dammit, it wasn't as if he'd invited his life to go into that downhill destructive spiral, it just had. And for the first time in years his cop instincts were telling him if he could just manage to put a couple of things together and look at the sum, he might have a shot at exorcizing some of the demons that haunted him day and night.

But he had zero chance to do that without the cooperation of the gorgeous redhead who was presently sitting in the driver's seat of her idling cruiser, watching him with guarded eyes the color of hard jade.

"There's something about Windsor's murder that I can't shake off," he began. "I don't *want* to shake it off because my gut is telling me to stay here and find out what that something is. That maybe if I do, I'll find some answers."

Liz tilted her head as if to gain a new perspective. "Answers to what?"

Why had just touching the Colt sent needles of edgy tension prickling through him? Sam thought for starters. *Why had the cop working the case brought back memories of the redheaded girl from his childhood dreams? And why the hell did he know without a doubt that Liz Scott needed protection?*

Sam suspected that voicing those questions would probably have her wondering if he was some psycho.

"Sometimes you don't know what answers you're looking for until you stumble across them," he answered vaguely. "All I know is that listening to my instincts has saved my butt uncountable times during my career. I'm not going to start ignoring them now."

Liz couldn't argue with that. Her own innate cop sixth sense had kept her safe many times over the years. But agreeing to let Sam Broussard work on the Windsor case seemed absurd when she thought about her complete physical response to him. Still, the instincts she had learned to trust were telling her to let him stay. That sending him away would be a huge mistake.

And she had no clue why.

Which was just one more item to add to her growing lists of unexplainable things and events.

"I'll talk to my boss," she said and shrugged. "You recovered the murder weapon, so that connects you to the Windsor homicide. If we make an arrest and the case goes to trial, you'll probably be called to testify about the Colt. It shouldn't be a problem to get approval for you to consult on this investigation with me."

Sam nodded the merest fraction. "I appreciate it."

"Just don't forget it's *my* investigation, Sam."

His gaze slid down her body, touching every part of her with a hot, melting look. Her face, her shoulders, her breasts.

Something dark came and went in his gaze. "I don't plan to cause you any problems, Liz."

Too late, she thought while her hammering pulse turned everything inside her hot and sensitive.

Too damn late.

Chapter 5

"Damn." Standing in the plush dressing room in the back of Silk & Secrets, Liz slid her cell phone into the pocket of her jade blazer. "Damn. *Damn!*"

Allie Fielding looked up from her drafting table where snippets of bright silk and delicate lace lay amid sketches of negligees, robes and bustiers. With manicured fingers, she brushed back the blond hair that waved over one cheek. "What's wrong? Did your boss turn down your request to let Detective Studly consult on the homicide case?"

"His name's Broussard. And Captain Ryan gave me the go-ahead."

"So, why the triple damns?"

"I want Broussard to leave."

Allie laid the sketch aside and swiveled on her long-legged stool to face Liz. Her tailored business suit in muted coral looked as fresh now as it had that morning.

"When Claire and I were with you at the bakery and Sam walked in, I could tell by the way you looked at him that something's going on."

"You're wrong, Al. There's *nothing* going on."

"Then why don't you want to work with him?"

Liz plopped down on the powder-pink love seat opposite the drafting table and took a slow drag of the lavender-scented air. "He...*bothers* me."

"Bothers, as in he cracks his knuckles? Or bothers you on a man/woman level?"

Liz shoved her thick braid behind one shoulder. She'd been heading to her loft when she glanced across Reunion Square and noticed the lights still on in Allie's shop. Figuring her friend had an after-hours appointment with one of her special clients, and feeling antsy and unsettled, Liz detoured across the square and rang the bell at the shop's front door. Only minutes after Allie let her in, Captain Ryan called to give the okay for Broussard to consult on the Windsor case.

Knowing she'd be working in close proximity with him for an unspecified amount of time had Liz feeling like a bomb ticking toward the blast.

"Broussard doesn't crack his knuckles," Liz muttered.

"So, it's the man/woman thing." Pink diamond earrings the size of small-caliber bullets glinted as Allie tilted her head. Liz knew the gems were a mere blip on the radar screen of the huge estate Allie Wentworth Fielding had inherited when her investment banker father passed away years ago.

"Sam Broussard is an attractive, sexy man with shoulders out to here." Allie threw her arms extravagantly wide. "The fact there's chemistry between you two might be a good thing."

"It's a *terrible* thing," Liz countered.

Frustration driving her, she rose and paced the length of the small, elegant dressing room, the thick silver carpet muffling her footsteps. "A little over two weeks ago I was engaged to Andrew. I'm still trying to figure out why I couldn't make myself walk down the aisle either time I tried to marry him. If that's not bad enough, a blue-eyed hunk whose face I've never seen and *'bewares'* me in some foreign language interrupts my sleep nightly for a bout of molten lava sex. Now, I'm close to getting the hots for an out-of-town cop who has somehow morphed into my new partner." Liz clenched her hands against her thighs. "Dammit, Allie, I don't *need* this."

"Then why did you ask your boss to let Studly work the case with you?"

"Because I'd be an idiot to turn down the offer of free help on this case—on any case—from an experienced investigator. And…" Without slowing her pacing, Liz threw up a hand in frustration. "I admit it—there's something inside me that couldn't say no to Broussard's offer. Something that wants him to stay."

"Maybe your subconscious is trying to tell you that

Sam is just who you need right now," Allie countered. "He's someone new. Someone you have no past with."

Zeroing in, Liz stopped midstep. "What makes you think I have a past with Dream Lover?"

Allie pursed her coral-glossed lips. "If you didn't know him, why would you dream about him?"

Liz frowned. "If I *know* him, why the heck can't I figure out who he is?"

Allie slid off her stool, crossed the thick carpet in an easy glide in skinny heels and squeezed her friend's arm. "Relax, Liz. Just go with the flow. See what, if anything, develops between you and Detective Studly."

Considering the way her heart rate picked up and her blood heated whenever she was around Broussard, Liz had a pretty good idea of what would develop, at least on her part.

Just then, the doorbell at the shop's front chimed.

Allie sighed. "I wish we could talk longer, but my client's here for her fitting."

"Not a problem." Liz knew that Allie saw several women whom she termed "special clients" after regular business hours. "So, who's on for tonight?"

"Mercedes."

Liz raised an eyebrow. "Isn't she the one who fell off your pinning platform wearing only a red teddy and stilettos? Hit her head and got carted off on a gurney by a couple of EMTs whose tongues were hanging to the floor?"

"The one and only." Allie rolled her eyes. "Mercedes also dropped a Waterford flute filled with Merlot when she fell. The glass shattered and the wine left a huge stain on the carpet. Since then, I serve my clients only white wine."

"You could make her come here while the shop's open so you wouldn't have to work late."

"And take a chance on Mercedes running into her sugar daddy's wife? I don't think so."

"Yeah, a catfight in the shop would be bad for business."

"Exceptionally bad."

Liz grabbed her tote off the love seat. "I'm going to duck out the back. I'll lock the door behind me."

"Okay." Allie headed toward the arched doorway that led to the shop, then paused and turned back toward Liz. "Are you going home now?"

Liz knew she could just call Broussard and tell him he was cleared to work the Windsor case. But since she had to walk past the inn on her way back to The Montgomery where she lived, it seemed cowardly not to tell him in person that they were officially temporary partners.

"I'll go home after I tell Broussard the news," she answered.

Allie's expression softened. "If you need to talk later, call me. Doesn't matter what time."

Her friend's concern made Liz's throat clog. "Thanks, Al. I'll keep that in mind."

Pebbles crunched under Sam's pounding feet as he jogged on the track behind the Reunion Square Inn. It was a clear moonlit night, the air crisp. His breath puffed out in white plumes, then rushed in, sharp and cold. Small lights on wrought-iron posts cast the narrow oval track in an aged yellow tint.

He'd run a couple of miles but hadn't pushed his pace, so his breathing was only slightly labored. There was a time he had forced himself to the limit, hammering his way through his daily ten-mile run in an attempt to exorcize demons. Having given up on those unsuccessful attempts at ridding himself of old ghosts, he now ran because the alternative—thinking about the past—did him no good. He couldn't change things. Couldn't go back and erase the starring role he'd played in his wife's death.

Couldn't rid himself of the guilt that burned inside him.

He'd just reached the side of the track farthest from the cozy brick inn when his mind flashed a warning he was no longer alone.

But this warning didn't put his cop-senses instantly on alert for it was accompanied by a thickening of his blood and a primal lust that shot through his belly. With it came the sudden awareness of who had triggered the warning. Somehow, someway he *felt* her.

And smelled her dark, tempting scent.

Halting abruptly, Sam turned. And Liz was there, standing on the opposite side of the track as if he'd conjured her up out of the night air. Beneath the lights her braided hair was a column of shimmering fire.

Watching her, Sam swiped at his brow with the

forearm of his sweatshirt. The fact he'd known someone was watching didn't surprise him—like most cops, he had an ingrained radar honed by years on the job. What he couldn't explain was how he'd instinctively known the watcher was Liz Scott.

"Christ," Sam muttered when he felt himself stir. His response to her was dangerous and, as the past with Tanya had taught him, potentially deadly. Which was why he forced himself to balance the tight throb of lust in his gut with caution. He wasn't going to repeat the mistakes he'd made that had been driven by blatant physical desire.

Desire that paled in comparison to what he felt when he paused a few feet from Liz and her scent seemed to pour over him until his belly ached and his head felt light. *Not good,* he thought. *Not at all good.*

"Evening, Liz."

"Sam."

Up close, he could see that her face was tight with strain. "Something wrong?"

"No. It's just that…" She glanced across her shoulder at the inn.

"It's just what?"

She remet his gaze. "I knew you were back here."

"Because the desk clerk told you where to find me?"

"No." She skimmed a thumb over the inside of her right wrist in a gesture that he now knew was habit. "I got to the inn's front porch when all of a sudden something told me you'd be back here. I had no idea you jogged, but somehow I *knew* I'd find you on this track." She shook her head. "How the hell would I know that?"

He remembered the jolt that had passed between them when they first shook hands. And the feeling of familiarity that had washed over him, a sensation that made him think their paths had crossed sometime in the past.

Then there were his childhood dreams of the red-headed girl. Dreams he'd forgotten all about until he met Liz Scott.

"If you figure it out, let me know," he said levelly. "Then maybe you can tell me how I knew you were here before I even spotted you."

"You sensed you were no longer alone?"

"That, but I also knew *you* were the reason I was no longer alone."

Her forehead furrowed. "How the hell would you know that?"

"I guess maybe the same way you knew where to find me."

He saw her shoulders lift beneath her jade blazer. "Maybe this is some sixth-sense-type deal? Sort of like when we don't have proof some scuzzball is lying, but we automatically know."

Sam thought of the list of things he had no explanation for that was as long as the rap sheet of a career criminal.

"Could be," he agreed while using his forearm to take another swipe at his damp forehead. "All I know for sure is that I don't want my Grandmother Broussard to get wind of this."

"Why? Think she'd round up your aunt and cousins and head to the churchyard to gather more nettles?"

"Only if one of us is suffering from dropsy," he said dryly. "In this instance, she'd put together an herb bag for each of us with instructions that we sleep with it under our pillow."

"An herb bag," Liz repeated, giving him an uncertain look. "Your grandmother sounds like an interesting woman."

"One of a kind," Sam replied.

Overhead, the moon was full. Pure white. Cool and full and promising. His gaze swept across Liz's alabaster skin, her wide-set emerald eyes and silky lashes.

Possessiveness coiled deep within him, a fierce, primitive thing that shocked him with its strength. He felt the air leave his lungs in a rush, as if he'd just run a marathon.

"So, Liz," he said after a moment. "Is this visit business or pleasure?"

"Business," she replied instantly. "I was at Allie's shop when my captain called. Since the inn is on my way home, I decided to stop by and let you know you're approved to consult on the Windsor investigation."

Relief swept through Sam. Now, he had a chance to find out what it was about this particular case—and the woman in charge of it—that had grabbed him by the throat and wouldn't let go.

"Glad to hear it," he said. "Did you make any progress on the case after you dropped me off here this afternoon?"

"Some. I found out J. D. Temple told us the truth

about his brother getting killed in a drive-by shooting. Hope you don't mind grunt work, Broussard, because tomorrow we're going to dig through the archives and try to find the reports on the one hundred burglaries Temple pled guilty to thirty years ago. Then we'll know if he lied when he claimed he never stole a gun."

"Grunt work doesn't bother me. And if it turns out Temple didn't take guns, that'll add credence to his claim about not lifting the Colt from York's house."

"If that's the case, we'll have to go back to the judge. Ask him to try to find some receipts so we'll know what company he hired to do renovations at his house a few weeks before the burglary."

Her mention of York reminded Sam of the almost atavistic dislike he'd felt for the man, which had been followed by the instinctive need to defend the woman who was now his partner for the foreseeable future. "I need to get up to speed on the Windsor case, so I'd like to go through the file as soon as possible." His gaze went to her bulging tote bag. "Do you have it with you?"

She nodded. "I'm going through it again tonight, see if I can find any leads I've overlooked. I also need to track down a family member of the now-deceased Oklahoma City fence. The one Temple claimed he sold the bracelet with the weird red stone to."

"How about you leave the file with me tonight?" Sam suggested. "That way, I'll be current on all the details by morning."

"Sorry," Liz said and Sam noted the imperceptible

tightening of her arm against her bag. "I don't let my work files out of my sight."

"Don't trust your new partner?"

"Temporary partner," she corrected. "And it's nothing personal."

Just then, the clock in the tower in the center of Reunion Square bonged. For reasons he couldn't explain, Sam felt a growing sense of urgency to find out all the details of Geneviève Windsor's murder.

"How about a compromise?" he suggested. "I'll come to your place for a couple of hours. That way we can both go through the file."

When he saw the hesitation in her eyes, he crossed his arms over his chest and grinned. "I promise to wipe my feet and mind my manners."

The breath she blew out as she laughed plumed into a gray cloud on the cold air. "All right." She glanced at her own watch. "But it's been a long day, so when I say it's time to shut things down, we shut them down. Deal?"

For Sam, the night suddenly seemed to close in, encasing them in darkness. Together. As her scent filled his lungs, he felt himself starting to reach out just as she stepped back, as if she may have felt it, too—that strange magnetic pull.

He clenched his hand into a fist. "It's a deal I can't turn down," he said quietly.

On The Montgomery's tenth floor, Sam followed Liz off the elevator into an airy loft apartment. The space was almost entirely open. Steel columns, each painted a soft dove-gray, supported a cavernous ceiling. Colorful rugs were scattered across the wood floor. There wasn't much furniture: a couch at an angle to a massive brick fireplace, chairs and tables, an eclectic collection of lamps. But what was there looked tasteful and expensive.

"Want some coffee while you look through the file?" Liz asked.

"Sounds good."

Sam's gaze flicked to the staircase painted the same gray as the columns. He figured Liz's bedroom was on the upper level, and he couldn't stop himself from wondering if she had spent even a few minutes lying in her bed overhead, thinking of him. Or was he the only one who'd lost sleep since they met?

He exhaled between his teeth. Time to refocus his thoughts. "Need some help?"

She gave him a level look as she paused beside the couch and dug the thick homicide file out of her tote bag. "Are you offering because someone at the P.D. clued you in that I'm a lousy cook?"

"No." The air in the loft was warm, prompting him to shove up the arms of his sweatshirt. "My grandmother taught me to always offer to lend a hand to my host or hostess."

"The more I hear about your grandmother, the more I like her." Liz shrugged out of her jade blazer, laid it neatly over the back of the couch. "Thanks, but I can manage a pot a coffee."

"Had to ask, Liz."

Sam watched her move toward the far end of the loft where a counter topped in gray granite separated the kitchen from the living area. With that sleek body and mile-long legs hugged by a dark sweater and slacks, she moved as fluidly as a dancer.

And he damn well wondered what those legs would feel like bare and wrapped around him.

With the thought shooting straight to his glands, he tore his gaze from her and stepped to the nearest window. Staring out into the night, Sam could feel the ache in his jaw that told him his teeth were clamped together. Where Liz Scott was concerned, he knew now he wasn't going to be able to stop himself from wanting her. Badly.

Dammit, he was here to work, he reminded himself. To try to make sense of what it was about the Windsor case that had him feeling antsy and unsettled. And, if his instincts were on target, he might wind up somehow protecting Liz. But that was it. Bottom line, he couldn't trust his emotions. So, as much as he wanted Liz, he was just as determined not to have her.

The instant Liz stepped around the counter and into the kitchen, she spotted the cardboard box. The cop in her stiffened from the knowledge someone had been in her loft while she was gone. But when she noted the handwriting on the envelope lying beside the box, the clenching of her heart overtook all other emotion. *Andrew.*

The note her ex-fiancé left was short and to the

point. He had found a few of her belongings at his condo, boxed them up and returned them, along with his key to her loft. The last item of business they had to deal with was emptying their joint safe-deposit box. Andrew would contact her to set up a time.

Tears stinging her eyes, Liz closed her palm over the key she shook out of the envelope. She'd been so happy when she gave it to Andrew, so sure she loved him, that he was the only man for her. Forever. How could something that at one time felt so right turn so terribly wrong?

"Liz?"

She jumped a little when Sam's voice came from a few inches away. Turning, she saw he was standing just behind her.

"You all right?"

"Yes. Why?"

"I always ask that question of someone who suddenly goes as pale as chalk." His gaze dropped to the envelope clenched between her fingers. "Your hands are trembling."

That was the problem with hanging around sharp-eyed detectives, Liz thought. You couldn't get a thing past them. She didn't think for one second Broussard had missed the tears she still struggled to hold back. He just hadn't mentioned them.

She knew she could tell him the source of her discomfort was personal, that it was none of his business. Which was true. But it wasn't just a cop's perception she saw in his silver-gray eyes. There was concern, too.

She gestured toward the box. "My ex-fiancé returned the things I had at his place."

Sam angled his head. "Guess Vegas will never hold good memories for either of you."

"Not just Vegas," Liz said. "Two weeks before we flew there, I stood in the rear of a church here while a kazillion wedding guests waited for me to walk down the aisle."

"Twice?" Sam asked, resting a hip against the counter. "You tried to marry the same guy two times? In two weeks?"

"Yes. I couldn't manage to walk down the aisle either time." Liz glided her fingertips along the top edge of the box. "I always thought getting through the wedding would be the easy part. That it was the actual marriage that took all the work."

"That was the way it was for me."

Her hand stilled against the box and she looked up. There was no expression at all in Sam's eyes now. Oh Lord, less than an hour ago she had watched him jogging, thinking how incredibly sexy he looked in gray sweatpants that clung to his taut butt. And about how his black sweatshirt had emphasized the muscled shoulders that Allie had described as amazing. Liz tried to swallow past the knot in her throat. Had she been standing on the jogging track, having lustful thoughts about a married man? If so, it was a wonder lightning hadn't struck her.

"You're married?" she asked, her voice barely a whisper.

"Was."

The breath she'd been holding seeped out of her lungs. "Okay."

"Look, it's understandable you're upset about how things turned out. But it sounds like there's something inside of you that knew marrying your fiancé would be a mistake. Considering the hell two people who aren't right for each other can create, you're better off in the long run."

From the steely tone that had crept into his voice, Liz suspected Sam's marriage had experienced its own particular hell.

She dropped the key back into the envelope, laid it on top of the box. Wanting a few minutes to get her emotions back on track, she pulled a can of coffee and a filter out of a cabinet, then turned to Sam.

"Mind getting a pot of this brewing while I take these things upstairs?"

"Be glad to."

"Thanks, I'll be right back."

"Liz," he said when she reached for the box.

The single word spoken in his deep Southern accent was full throated, as lazy and sexy as black silk. And had her nerves humming.

"Yes?"

"If you need some time alone, I'll go. Geneviève Windsor's been dead thirty years. I can wait until morning to review the murder file."

His face was close enough to see the dark outer rim of his iris, and to count, if she had the urge, his inky-black lashes.

How, she wondered, could she be upset over her ex-fiancé, and at the same time react to the ruggedly handsome cop whose mere presence was playing havoc with her pulse rate? He might not have his hands on her, but she had the sensation that his silvery-gray eyes were touching her instead. "You're here now," she said, while fighting the shudder in her blood. "We might as well work."

"What's the count?" Sam asked the following afternoon while shifting for the umpteenth time in his chair beside Liz's. "How many more old reports do we have left to find?"

She slid him a look. They had already logged several hours at the microfilm readers in the cubbyhole off the basement archives room that was even more of an airless murky cave than her own office down the hall. In truth, the impatience she felt equaled his, but she wasn't going to admit that. Not when her unease had little to do with their present task and everything to do with her inability to erase from her head last night's image of him sitting beside her at her kitchen counter.

He had said very little after they started reviewing the Windsor file. When Sam had spoken, it was to ask a question or make a comment pertaining to the homicide.

After he reviewed the final report, he closed the file folder and rose. He rinsed out his coffee mug, said good-night and left.

Hours later, she had jolted awake, her body trembling in the throes of completion and the remembered feel of Dream Lover's hands against her flesh. Muffling a curse, she'd dragged a pillow across her face and tried to block out the thought that, in reality, the man she wanted sharing her bed was Sam Broussard.

"How many more, you figure?" he asked again before easing his chair farther back from the table on which the microfilm reader sat. When he shifted to stretch out his long legs, she caught a whiff of his spicy aftershave.

The warmth that zinged up her spine had Liz setting her jaw. She'd thought they would locate copies of the reports faster on the one hundred burglaries J. D. Temple had confessed to if she and Broussard worked at separate readers at the same time. *Idiotic idea,* she now realized. It was bad enough she had last night's image of him tape-looping through her brain. To make matters worse, each time he reached to press the print button on his reader, her gaze zeroed in on his long-fingered, bronze-skinned hand. And her thoughts veered to wondering if those fingers would feel as hard and possessive against her bare flesh as Dream Lover's had.

Liz felt her spine stiffen as the implications of that thought sunk in. How could she know what Dream Lover's touch felt like if he was a fantasy? That made as much sense as her "knowing" Sam had been behind the inn on the track last night.

"Liz?"

"I don't know how many!" she shot back, whipping her face toward him.

One of his dark brows quirked. "You're the one keeping the list of the reports we've located and printed." He studied her for a long moment. "Sounds like you're enjoying this chore as much as I am."

"Sorry, I'm just tired."

"You have a restless night?"

"You might call it that." She shoved one hand under her braid to rub at the knots of tension in her neck. "Look, I told you if you worked with me there would be grunt work involved."

"And I told you I didn't have a problem with that. Doesn't mean I enjoy searching through hazy films of thirty-year-old burglary reports until my eyes glaze."

Just the way his flinty gaze locked with hers had her nerves spiking. If she didn't create some space between them, she was going to jump out of her skin.

"All right, change of plans. When you went through the Windsor file, you said you couldn't find Max Hogan's military records. Why don't you go back to the office and start the wheels turning on getting a copy?" She nodded toward the reader in front of her. "I'll finish up here."

"All right. First, though, I'm curious about something."

"What?"

"That mark on your wrist."

Liz slid her hand from the back of her neck. "What about it?"

She nearly jolted when he wrapped his fingers

lightly around her wrist. "Is it a scar or a birthmark?" he asked, lifting her arm for a better look.

"Birthmark."

When he tilted her wrist toward the room's stingy lights and leaned in, Liz had a close-up view of the strong, tanned column of his throat. Of the open collar of his denim work shirt that revealed dark, crisp hair. She couldn't control the shiver that raced beneath her flesh. The man was going to give her heart failure.

"Does it bother you?"

"Bother me?" she echoed, aware that her voice was as unsteady as her pulse rate.

"You rub it a lot." As if to demonstrate, he swept his thumb along the inner side of her wrist. "Like maybe it aches at times."

"I…" She dragged in an unsteady breath. She couldn't shake the feeling of familiarity as he stroked her flesh. It was the identical feeling she'd had when he looked down at her during her whoo-hoo episode at the apartment building. Like she'd encountered Sam Broussard sometime in the past. But that was impossible.

"It's an unconscious habit," she managed. "One of my foster mothers swore I'd wear away my skin."

"Foster *mothers,*" Sam repeated, his gaze lifting from her wrist. "How long were you in the system?"

"Since the day I was found in a basket of dirty clothes at a self-service laundry. I was about a week old."

"Sounds like you had a rough go of things."

"I managed."

"How many foster homes were you in?"

"Too many to count."

He looked at her thoughtfully. "A lot of kids who get moved around are rebels."

"Which is a polite term for 'troublemaker.' You asking if I caused trouble, Sam?"

"You couldn't have done anything too serious since you wound up being a cop."

"True." Liz furrowed her brow against the unease trickling through her. She seldom talked about her past, had no idea why she was now telling a man she barely knew about it. But for some reason, talking to him seemed right.

"I was always in homes with other foster kids and no matter how badly they'd been treated—even abused—most tried to behave and toe the line because they wanted to reunite with their real family. I didn't have anyone to go back to so I didn't try to put on an act. If I didn't like someone or something, I let people know. That labeled me a 'rebel' and the minute I proved inconvenient, I was out on my butt and on my way to another foster home."

"How'd you wind up pinning on a badge?"

"One of the last case workers I got assigned to was a retired cop. She'd grown up in foster care, too, and I guess she saw a little of herself in me. She took me under her wing, steered me in the direction of law and order."

When his thumb made another light sweep across her inner wrist, Liz tugged from his hold.

"Look, it's just a birthmark. No big deal." She barely got the words out. Her body was aware—*very aware*—of his nearness, responding to it in ways that were instinctive and fundamentally feminine—warming, melting. With a wall on one side of her and Broussard on the other, she was caught between an immovable object and an irresistible force. When he lifted a hand to stroke the column of her braid, her eyes went wide.

"Your hair looks like it would be warm to the touch," he murmured, lowering his head inch by inch.

He was going to kiss her. She knew it; she could read the intention in his eyes, could see the dark longing that matched her own.

She should have moved. She should have stopped him. The events of the past weeks had left her emotions raw. There were too many things happening in her life that she was at a loss to understand. The last thing she needed was to jump into an affair. Besides, Sam was officially her partner and one of her ironclad rules was to never get involved with a cop she worked with. He had no business touching her and she had no business wanting him to.

Her heartbeat revved with the urgency of a junkie craving a fix. She held her breath, waiting, watching, as his mouth drew closer.

She should have stopped him.

But she didn't.

Chapter 6

When Sam's lips grazed hers, Liz didn't protest. She didn't lean away. She wasn't sure she continued to breathe. Not when every emotion she had felt since the instant he walked into her office a mere few days ago meshed into one: desire. Unexplainable. Unbeatable. Unquenchable.

His fingers were still curved around her wrist, warm and heavy against her flesh. In the drab light of the P.D.'s small microfilm room his eyes were so smoky-gray, so intense, that for a moment she blinked, assaulted by a powerful sense of déjà vu.

But she'd never been this close to Sam Broussard before, she assured herself. Never before felt his lips skim her jawline as they did now, spiking her pulse and leaving her dazed and drunk and desperate.

Too desperate.

With an effort, she thrust the heel of one hand against his shoulder, and felt the corded strength in him as she eased back in her chair. Fighting to catch her breath, she stared at Sam and saw the hunger that gripped her mirrored in his eyes.

The knowledge his desire matched hers played havoc with her fast-shredding common sense. What kind of power did he have, she wondered, that he could turn her from a sensible, responsible woman into a trembling puddle of need?

"We're on duty," she managed. "We just broke about five rules."

"Yeah." Releasing his hold on her wrist, he stabbed his fingers through his dark hair. "Maybe more."

She flicked a look across the room. The door stood ajar; beyond it was the huge archives storage area that was staffed by two civilian employees. Liz heard no voices or nearby footsteps drifting in on the still air. Thankfully there were no witnesses to their blatant disregard for departmental policy.

"Guess we dodged a bullet," Sam said, as if reading her mind.

"Lucky for us." Sitting so close beside him made Liz feel caught. Defenseless. Out of control.

Going on the defensive, she shoved her chair away from her microfilm reader and rose. It was way past time to set the ground rules. For them both.

"Look, Sam, despite what just happened, I don't get involved with my coworkers."

"Neither do I."

"Okay. Good." She scrubbed at the inside of her right wrist, frowning when she realized heat had pooled where his fingers had lain. "Then we're agreed. Nothing like this can happen between us again."

"I take my career as serious as you do yours." Sam rose, faced her. "I didn't plan on kissing you, it just happened. And I agree, nothing like this *should* happen again." He paused for a split second. "At least not while we're on duty. But something's going on. There's a connection between us that I can't explain."

She felt herself go still. Had he experienced the same type of déjà vu moments she had? "What sort of connection?"

"That first day in your office I mentioned that you look familiar. I can't shake the feeling we've met before, but I can't tag where or when."

"That's because we've never met." What woman could forget a man who was six feet of solid muscle with a linebacker's shoulders, firm square jaw and steely-gray eyes?

Eyes that were now narrowed and focused on her face. "Are you sure?"

Then there was that low, rich Louisiana accent that made her pulse jump. Never before had a man's voice had the power to send energy flowing through every cell in her body. "Positive."

"What about you?" His brows pulled together in

frustration, he stepped toward her but didn't reach out. "Have you had the same feeling about me? That our paths crossed sometime in the past?"

She wanted to tell him no, but she couldn't deny her own déjà vu moments—including the sense of familiarity she'd felt when his lips brushed against hers. "I've…had a couple of the same type of sensations as you."

He gave a brusque nod. "And don't forget about last night when you knew I was on the jogging track, and I knew you were there, too."

"I thought we agreed to write that off as a cop's sixth sense."

"Even so, I've got a lot of questions. And at this point, not one damn answer."

Liz's cell phone rang. With a hand that wasn't quite steady, she dug the phone out of the pocket of her wool jacket, checked the display.

"I need to take this call from a stolen goods detective," she told Sam. "He's trying to get a line on a relative of the fence who J. D. Temple claims he sold the bracelet with the red stone to."

Sam blew out a breath. "I'll go back to the office and get started on the request for those military records."

Liz answered the call. And waited until Sam disappeared out the door to squeeze her eyes shut.

It was hard to think with every nerve in her body on shivering edge. Which was why she was imagining things, she assured herself. Why she was totally mistaken to think that one soft brush of Sam Broussard's mouth against hers had felt anywhere as electrifying as Dream Lover's.

When Sam returned to the cold case office, he settled at the table Liz had commandeered as his work area for the duration of their partnership.

Instead of obtaining the military records of the marine who'd died alongside Geneviève Windsor, Sam leaned back in his chair and closed his eyes, hoping to blot out the memory of Liz's wary, expressive face. He couldn't begin to understand the impact she had on him, so powerful it overrode his better judgment and what he'd believed was a self-control equivalent to steel.

Granted, he wanted her, and there was nothing rational or civilized about it. Not when he felt agitated and primitive enough to toss her over his shoulder and carry her off to the nearest bed. Or storage closet. Or floor.

"Christ," he muttered, scrubbing a hand over his face. His marriage had spiraled into a black hole and he readily accepted part of the blame. He'd had his heart ripped out and was shouldering a ton of guilt for the role he'd played in Tanya's murder.

Since then, all he'd been interested in were one-night stands. *No* strings, no ties.

Where Liz Scott was concerned, he knew one time wouldn't be enough. Not even close. For a man who'd been to hell and hadn't made it all the way back, he should be putting distance between himself and Liz. Instead he was thinking that if he didn't get his hands on her soon he was going to explode.

With frustration rippling inside him, Sam grabbed the phone and got to work.

That frustration still clung to him hours later when he and Liz made their way into a pawnshop.

The woman behind the counter was in her early fifties, with crow's feet radiating from the corners of her eyes. Tall and big-boned with bottle-blond hair that showed darker roots, she wore jeans and an oversize red sweater. After flicking a look from Liz to Sam, then back again, she frowned.

"Are you guys cops?"

"You pegged us." Liz nudged aside one flap of her wool jacket to reveal her badge. "I'm Sergeant Scott, this is Detective Broussard. Are you Sunny Clymer?"

"Yeah." She studied them warily. "I run an honest operation here. If I think a piece of merchandise is stolen, I don't take it in."

Sam spared a jaded look at nearby shelves bulging with tools, electronics and sporting goods, about half of the items in their original box. He figured a run of serial numbers on the merchandise would get a number of stolen hits.

"We're not here to talk about how you do business," Liz said. "Are you Vic Dunn's daughter?"

"Yes." Clymer gestured with a hand sparkling with various diamond rings. "He's been dead for twenty years, so you're out of luck if you want to talk to him."

"It's you we came to see," Liz said. "We understand you used to work with him in his fencing operation."

"Flea market business," Clymer corrected with a

straight face. "Dad never knowingly involved himself in any illegal business deals."

Sam sensed Liz was having to bite her tongue to hold back. Dunn had been busted numerous times for possession of stolen property. But he and Liz wanted information from the woman—no reason to antagonize her by casting aspersions on her old man.

"Does the name J. D. Temple ring a bell?" Liz asked.

"Hell, yeah." Her mouth curving, Clymer pulled a pack of cigarettes from under the counter and lit up. She took a drag, released the smoke. "When I was working with my dad at the flea market booth, J.D. was a regular customer. He was a nice man, always had a joke to tell. And he had a memory like a steel trap." Clymer squinted behind a fresh cloud of smoke. "I guess if you're here asking about him, you know where he is?"

"He earned himself an extended stay at the state pen."

Clymer shook her head. "That's a shame."

Liz pulled a piece of paper out of her pocket, unfolded it and laid it on the counter in front of Clymer. "Temple claims he sold your father a gold cuff bracelet that looks something like this. The stone in its center is red. We're looking for any records that might prove Temple's claim."

"All the records Dad kept are long gone." Clymer tapped an inch-long, gem-studded fingernail against the sketch. "But I don't need them to tell you about this bracelet. I remember it."

"From thirty years ago?"

"Yeah."

Sam took a step closer to Liz and felt his gut tighten. He had studied the sketch a couple of times, but that was before today in the microfilm room when he got a close-up look at Liz's inner right wrist. It hit him now that the bracelet's lattice weave design had a similar pattern as her birthmark.

How could that be anything other than coincidence? he wondered and frowned when a murky scene swam into his consciousness.

A young woman with fiery hair flowing from beneath a hooded cloak, fleeing through the cold mist. A dark-haired man with black-as-pitch eyes and a bloody sword.

"You can't tell it from J.D.'s sketch," Clymer continued, "but the stone wasn't a solid red color. It had dark streaks running through it. Like veins."

Baffled and uneasy with the image that had every protective instinct inside him rearing up, Sam shook it off. "Like veins, under the skin?" he asked.

"Right."

He looked at Liz. And sensed that, like him, she was thinking about Temple's comment that the stone had seemed alive.

Clymer tipped her head back and blew out smoke. "To this day, I remember the weight of the bracelet in my hand. Dad said it was eighteen carat gold. He had no idea what kind of gem the stone was, though."

"Over the years, your father must have dealt with thousands of pieces of jewelry," Liz said. "What was so special about this bracelet that you remember it?"

"That stone," Clymer answered. "There was just something about it that drew you. The bracelet was so distinctive, Dad decided not to sell it. Instead he planned on giving it to my mom for her birthday."

"Does your mother still have the bracelet?"

"Dad never got the chance to give it to her. Two days before her birthday, some thug wearing a ski mask grabbed him at closing time when he stepped out the back door of the flea market. Put a knife to Dad's throat, forced him back inside and threatened to kill Dad if he didn't turn over the bracelet with the red stone. Which he did."

Liz nodded slowly. "What other property did the robber take?"

"None. He didn't even give what was in the booth a second look. That didn't make sense, considering all the jewelry, coins and electronics Dad always had on hand."

"Did your father report the robbery?"

"Hell, no." Clymer shrugged. "Dad didn't have much use for cops."

With the phone lodged between her cheek and shoulder, Liz jotted notes at her desk. "So, Mr. Deakins, you had a revolver in the same drawer as your stamp collection?" she asked the man on the other end of the line. "The burglar took the stamps, but left the gun behind?"

"That's correct, Sergeant." The elderly man's voice was so high-pitched it was in the Pinocchio range. "I thought at the time that must have been an incredibly stupid thief. My Smith & Wesson was brand-new, he could have sold it on the street for a tidy sum."

"Crooks aren't known for their IQs," Liz said before thanking the man and ending the call.

Over the past days, she and Sam had located close to half the victims of the one hundred burglaries J. D. Temple had confessed to. Which was remarkable, considering the contact information off the burglary reports was thirty years old. Numerous victims verified they owned guns, some which were in plain sight of other property Temple had taken. But in no instance had any of the firearms been stolen.

Which convinced Liz that J. D. Temple had told the truth when he claimed he never stole a gun during his long career of breaking and entering. Nor had he taken the Colt from David York's house that later killed Geneviève Windsor.

At this very moment, Sam was upstairs, picking up a copy of the lab report that stated Temple's DNA didn't match the human tissue found inside the Colt. All those facts combined went a long way to clear the burglar of murder.

Functioning on too little sleep from Dream Lover's

nightly forays into her mind, Liz leaned back in her chair.

Something was bugging her about last night's dream. An uneasiness, or maybe even an awareness, had settled into her brain, but she couldn't grab onto it. All she knew was that there'd been some new element to Dream Lover's latest visit.

Resigned that whatever it was had been lost in the murky recesses of her mind, she shifted her thoughts back to the Windsor case. It was time to go back to square one, she decided.

It now looked likely that one of the construction crew who worked at York's house had lifted the Colt from the desk in the judge's study. York simply hadn't noticed the automatic was gone until weeks later when he returned from vacation to a burglarized house.

If the judge couldn't dig up the name of the construction company he hired thirty years ago, Windsor's murder might never be solved.

Which was something Liz didn't want to even think about. Nor was she willing to consider the possibility she shared some sort of weird cosmic connection with the cop who recovered the murder weapon.

Two days had passed since their grazing kiss in the microfilm room. Since then, they'd walked on eggshells around each other, each making sure to avoid all physical contact.

Their purposeful behavior might keep them on the right side of departmental policy, but it did nothing to quell the heat that pooled beneath Liz's flesh whenever Sam got near.

"Sergeant Scott?"

She glanced up to find David York standing in the open doorway of her office. The judge's gray suit fit his tall, whiplike form with tailored perfection, his starched dress shirt was snow-white, his tie dark crimson. Again she was struck by the stunning contrast between his silver hair and dark eyes.

The overall effect was one of power and authority.

"Your honor." As she rose, her thoughts veered to the possessiveness she'd felt in his handshake when she and Sam interviewed York in his chambers. And the resulting shudder of unease that swept through her.

Wanting to avoid contact, she slipped her hands into the pockets of her black slacks. "Welcome to the cold case office." When he stepped through the door, she nodded toward the lone visitor chair. "Have a seat."

"I had an appointment with your chief," York said, his voice deep and cultured. "So I took a chance on finding you here."

Instead of taking the seat she offered, York let his dark gaze sweep the office. "When I secured the federal grant to fund this unit, I had envisioned it would have more space. A window or two at least."

"That was the plan. I asked for a basement office instead."

"Indeed." York cocked his head, studying her. "Why?"

"The department's archives are just down the hall.

That's where the unsolved cases are filed. I wanted quick access to my assignments."

"Understandable. I'm sure you're aware that the renewal of the grant after the first year depends on the percentage of cases you clear. Now that I've met you, I have no doubt you have the tenacity to succeed."

"I plan on giving it my best shot," Liz said, her gaze tracking York's to the table against the only wall not lined with file cabinets. The file folders strewn across its top spoke of Sam's disregard for organization.

"The detective who came to my chambers with you." York looked back at her, his expression benign. "I believe his name was Broussard?"

"That's right."

"Has he returned to Louisiana?"

"Not yet. He's since found evidence that the man who burglarized your home spent time in Shreveport. Broussard is looking into the crimes the burglar confessed to here to see if he can match his M.O. to open cases there."

"And the unsolved homicide you mentioned?" York asked. "The one where the woman was killed with a .45. Do you still suspect the man who broke into my home may have murdered her with my Colt?"

"That's one possibility, but there are others. In fact, I planned on contacting you about that today."

"How so?"

"You said before you went on vacation you had work done on your home. That it's possible one of the workmen took the Colt from your desk weeks before the burglary occurred."

"That's correct. As I told you, I gave that information to the detective assigned to my case."

"His report on that didn't make it into the file. I realize we're talking about thirty years ago, but is there a chance you might have the name of the construction company you hired written down somewhere? On an old receipt, maybe?"

"Anything's possible, Sergeant." York's eyes stayed on hers. "I'll go through my files and check, then let you know."

"That'd be great." Liz retrieved one of her business cards from the holder on her desk. "You can contact me at any of these numbers if you find the name of the company."

York slid the card into the pocket of his suit coat. "I have a confession, Sergeant. Seeing the cold case office was just one of the reasons I stopped by."

"What was the other?"

"I wanted to personally deliver an invitation."

Unconsciously Liz rubbed the inside of her right wrist. "An invitation?"

"I do." York reached into the inside pocket of his suit coat and pulled out a square envelope. "Have you heard of the Committee of One Hundred?"

"Sure. It's a group made up mostly of civic leaders who do good things for the community."

"I've belonged to the organization since its inception. In fact, the grant I wrote for this office was sponsored by the committee. A week from today, we're having a reception to acknowledge the progress we've made over the past year. Your chief received an invitation, too. Unfortunately he has a prior engagement. But he said he would have you attend in his place to represent the department. As my guest, of course."

Great, Liz thought as she opened the envelope and slid out the heavy embossed card. The possibility that York's "attend as my guest" remark meant he wanted a date sent a shudder sprinting down her spine. She hunched her shoulder blades against it and forced her mouth to curve. "I'll see you there, Judge."

Sam heard Liz's comment at the same instant he stepped inside the cold case office. When he spotted York standing only inches from her, Sam had a fast, turbulent impulse to reach for his weapon.

Instead he tightened his fingers on the lab report he'd picked up while loathing rose in his chest. *Feeling must be mutual,* he thought when his gaze locked with York's and a flicker of annoyance marred the judge's smooth features.

"Detective Broussard."

"Judge York."

"It's a pleasure to see you again," York said then looked back at Liz. "Both of you. Now, I must get back to my courtroom."

The moment he disappeared down the hallway, Sam shoved the door closed. "What did he want?"

Liz's eyes narrowed at his sharp tone. "To check out my office, among other things. Since he was here, I asked York to dig through his old records to try to find the name of the construction company. He said he would."

Giving her a curt nod, Sam stalked to the table that served as his desk and tossed the report on top of the disarrayed paperwork. He had no clue why York's very presence started his early-warning system clanging like crazy. But every cop instinct Sam had developed after years on the job told him not to ignore his unease about the judge.

He moved back toward Liz's desk. "I heard you tell him 'I'll see you there.' Where the hell's there?"

She eyed him thoughtfully. "At a reception sponsored by a civic committee he belongs to. The group put muscle behind getting the federal grant that funds this office approved. Apparently the chief wants me to go as the department's representative."

"You're not going without me."

The remark, issued with cold and savage control, brought her chin up. "You'd be wise to back off that macho act right now, Broussard."

"It's not an act. There's something about York that doesn't sit right with me." Sam fisted his hands at his sides. "You shouldn't be around the guy alone. I can't tell you how I know that, I just do."

"Is this about that protection thing again?" As she spoke, Liz's hand settled on the automatic holstered at her waist. "You think I don't know how to handle myself?"

"I think in every instance you do. But somehow, someway, York changes things."

"That doesn't make sense."

When she started to turn toward her desk, Sam gripped her arms, held her still.

"I don't give a damn if it makes sense or not. All I care about is keeping you safe. Alive."

"Alive?"

He gazed down into her green eyes that he could have sworn he'd looked into a lifetime ago. "I don't have any answers," he said levelly. "I don't know what it is about York that sets off my cop vibes. But something tells me I need to protect you."

She looked at him, exasperated. "From *what?*"

"I wish to hell I knew." He tightened his fingers on her arms. "We've agreed there's some sort of connection between us. Even if it's just our cop instinct working overtime it's there. And York's a part of it."

He could almost see the thought processes behind Liz's eyes as she considered his words. And beneath his hands, he felt the tension in her arms ease.

"Look, I agree there's something off about York," she said. "But I don't get the same type of feeling about him that you do."

"What type do you get?"

"A creepy one. Like his thoughts turn lecherous when he looks at me. There's no way I'd forget if he and I had crossed paths before."

"Just like you and I have never met. Or don't remember meeting."

But they had, Sam thought. He was convinced of that now. Somehow, someway, Liz had played a part in his past. And, dammit, he wanted her in his present and maybe even his future.

But Tanya had been a part of his past, too. He had failed as a husband and a protector, and as a result, gotten his wife killed. Now here he was, a man whose soul had been stripped bare, trying to convince another woman he could shield her from danger.

The sorry truth was, he couldn't trust himself to be there for Liz, and she shouldn't, either. With a hollow feeling gnawing deep in his gut, he ran his hands down her arms before releasing them.

"Even though we don't remember meeting in the past, we both sense we have." Needing to put space between them, he moved to his work table, rested a hip on its edge. "Remember in his chambers how York got an astonished look on his face? Then seconds later he turned pale?"

"I remember. He claimed it was due to the building's heating system working overtime."

"Or, maybe he reacted that way because something familiar about one or both of us suddenly hit him? At this point, we shouldn't discount anything."

"Not when we're investigating a murder," Liz agreed. She scooped an envelope off her desk, walked the few steps to Sam and handed it to him. "Check your social schedule. If you're free, and still feel the need to provide backup, you can crash the reception."

He didn't bother to glance at the date. "I'm free," he said and passed the invitation back to her.

"What about tonight?"

He had a quick vision of what he'd like to do to Liz—*with her*—tonight and every night that followed. "What did you have in mind, Sergeant?"

"Work, Detective," she said, keeping her gaze level with his. "Remember my friend Claire Castle?"

"She owns the antique shop in Reunion Square, right?"

"Right. She sells antique jewelry in her shop. She has reference books on vintage jewelry, and she's okay with our dropping by after the shop closes this evening and taking a look at those books."

Sam crossed his arms over his chest. "You're thinking about the bracelet J. D. Temple swears he stole from York's house. That we might spot something similar in one of Claire's books."

"And maybe something on the red stone, too. A gem with veins running through it sounds distinctive. I'd like to know what the heck it is." Liz's gaze tracked to the office's closed door. "And why York didn't list the bracelet with the other property stolen from his house."

"That's just one of many questions we need to find the answer to," Sam said, then checked his watch. "What about dinner? Want to grab something to eat on our way to Claire's shop?"

"She and her husband, Jackson, have an apartment above the shop. We're invited to dinner, too."

Sam lifted a brow. "*We're* invited?"

"Claire made sure to extend you an invitation." Liz

lifted a shoulder. "You're on your own, new in town, she didn't want you to have to eat alone."

"That's nice of her."

"I have nice friends."

Sam let his gaze track down Liz's cheek, to the slender arch of her throat, made bare with her red-gold hair slicked back into an intricate braid. His gaze continued downward—with a few layovers—all the way to the toes of her sensible shoes, then back up again. As far as he was concerned, she had nice everything.

And she was his partner, whom he'd agreed to keep his hands off of. Still, nothing could dim his awareness of her. It was as if some force hung in the air, sweltering between them. A force that was old, and familiar.

So familiar, that he knew without a doubt that Liz Scott was somehow already his.

Chapter 7

That evening, Sam strode to the entrance of Home Treasures. His gaze swept across the Closed sign in the antique shop's window before he leaned a shoulder against the doorjamb and folded his arms over his chest.

Dusk was just now settling in. The carriage lights lining the sidewalk flicked to life, illuminating Reunion Square in a warm glow.

He checked the clock in the old brick tower in the square's center. When he and Liz left the cold case office, they had agreed to meet at six o'clock. In the meantime, he'd headed to his room at the inn while she drove off to run errands after assuring him she'd be at Claire and Jackson Castle's place on time.

True to her word, he thought seconds later when he spotted Liz walking across Reunion Square from her loft at The Montgomery.

His gaze swept down her, then up. He noted she'd changed into snug jeans, a plum-colored sweater and a short black leather jacket that hugged her lean body. And he took time to appreciate her unhurried walk that gave an elegant sort of swing to her denim-clad hips. But his attention riveted on the way her long hair draped across her shoulders like skeins of copper silk. As her steps brought her closer, light from the nearby lamps made that tumble of hair shine like wet fire.

He wasn't prepared for the sudden impact of sensation, like a punch in the stomach. How many times had he imagined himself unplaiting the braid she perpetually wore? Now, here she was with that mass of hair long and free and within touching distance. All he wanted was to bury his face in it.

"Hey, Sam."

He shut down his thoughts with a silent curse. "Liz. Get your errands run?"

"Mostly." The light breeze whipped her hair against her cheek. She swept a hand beneath it and scooped it across one shoulder. "Did you get all your stuff done?"

"Yeah." Considering the heat pumping inside him, he was sorry now he hadn't opted for cold water in the shower he'd taken after his ten-mile run.

She eased her hand into the front pocket of her jeans. As the denim pulled tight against her thighs, he felt his gut knot. *Should have taken two cold showers,* he amended.

A key emerged from the pocket. "Claire gave me this so neither she nor Jackson have to come down and let me in when I drop by."

"Guess they think you're trustworthy."

She gave him a smug smile before turning her attention to the lock. "I'm a lot of things, Broussard."

Including the most tempting woman he'd ever met.

The ache inside him didn't lessen when they walked through the cozy shop filled with antiques that glowed in the light of lamps turned low, then went upstairs to have drinks with Claire and Jackson Castle and Allie Fielding. Or while he sat beside Liz at dinner, his lungs filled with her tormenting scent while he made small talk with her friends. All the while he thought about plunging his fingers into those fiery strands and dragging her off to someplace dark and private where they could spend the next ten years alone.

For Sam, it was a relief when dinner ended and he wound up talking one-on-one with Jackson Castle.

"I've got some whiskey that'll add a kick to that brew if you're interested," Castle said while handing Sam a mug of coffee across the counter that separated the kitchen from the living room.

The man was tall with dark hair and a build that looked hard-edged and physical in a way that suggested an aggressively active lifestyle. According to Liz, lethal self-defense tactics was just one of the subjects Castle taught at Oklahoma City's Institute for the Prevention of Terrorism.

"Thanks, but I'd better pass," Sam said. "Liz and I still need to go through the books on antique jewelry your wife brought up from her shop."

Castle canted his head toward the opposite end of the spacious, high-ceilinged apartment. "Looks like if you play your cards right, you'll get to sidestep that job."

Sam shifted his gaze to where Liz, Claire and Allie had settled on the brightly floral couch and matching chairs in front of the blazing fireplace. Each woman had pulled a book off the stack on the coffee table and was leafing through it while they talked quietly among themselves.

Leaning against the counter, Sam sipped his coffee while studying Liz's profile. Surrounded by her friends, she looked content, her skin glowing in the firelight.

Just watching her had the need inside him deepening. If his desire for her grew any hotter, he'd burn to a crisp.

"How's it going, working with Liz?"

Jackson's question had Sam shutting down those thoughts. "So far, we haven't stepped on each other's toes."

Jackson sipped his coffee. "In law enforcement, having a good rhythm with your partner is always a plus." His gaze went to Claire. "Come to think of it, that applies to more than just cop work."

"You've got that right," Sam said under his breath. All evening, he'd been keenly aware of the easy, intimate affection that settled in Castle's eyes when the man gazed at his wife. Had *he* ever looked at Tanya that way? Sam wondered. He didn't think so.

"I worked a couple of unsolved investigations while I was an agent with the state department," Castle said. "But nothing close to a thirty-year-old unsolved murder. Takes a lot of deep digging into the past, I imagine."

"Yeah." The past, Sam thought, held the answer to who killed Geneviève Windsor. Something told him it was also where he and Liz would find an explanation for the inexplicable connection they felt to each other.

As Liz flipped through the pages of a book, she knew Sam was watching her. He stood all the way across the living room, sharing man-talk with Jackson Castle, yet she could feel that hard-as-granite gray gaze locked on her.

Keeping her attention on the pages of the large book on her lap, she fisted a hand against her stomach in an attempt to quell the nerves that had started humming when she arrived outside Home Treasures and spotted Sam waiting for her. He'd looked more rugged than refined in black jeans, a tan sweater and scarred bomber jacket. His gaze had swept down her and she'd felt as if he'd stripped her naked. There'd been something hot and not altogether civilized in his eyes that had put a weird jangling in her system.

Liz Scott, who'd disarmed vicious felons single-handedly and prided herself on being afraid of nothing, had found herself oddly frightened of Sam Broussard.

No, that wasn't right, she realized now that she'd had time to analyze her response. It wasn't *Sam* she was afraid of, but herself. And the edgy, out-of-control feelings that had bombarded her since she'd seen that feral look in his eyes.

Was there a woman alive who wouldn't feel desire licking at her veins when a man looked at her like that? Now, all she wanted to do was jump his bones.

"So, Liz, have you remembered more of what Dream Lover says to you?" Allie Fielding asked from the other end of the couch. Allie, dressed in black slacks and a silvery silk blouse, kept her voice low so that only Liz and Claire were privy to their conversation.

"Or at least figured out what language he's speaking?" Claire added from one of the chairs angled beside the couch.

Liz shook her head. "I still just remember him saying bewared. And toosh or tush. But there was something different about last night's dream. It's been eating at me all day."

Allie leaned in. "What?"

"I can't remember…." Liz's voice trailed off as the dark phantom of a memory stirred in her mind. And when that memory gelled, a chill shot up her spine.

"He had a gun," she said, forcing the words past the sudden tightness in her throat. "Last night, Dream Lover had a gun."

"Did he point it at you?" Allie asked, her eyes widening. "Threaten you?"

"I don't know." The confused, fragmented remnants of the dream hurtled around in Liz's brain. "All I could see were his blue eyes, like always." She raked her fingers through her hair. "But this time, he lifted his hand. Moonlight glinted off the gun's barrel." She paused, struggling to remember more, but there was nothing. "I must have woken up right then."

"I wonder what it means," Claire said. "That he had a gun when he never did before?"

"I wish to hell I knew." Her frustration mounting, Liz began fanning through the book's pages that displayed pictures of various gem-encrusted pieces of jewelry. If there was some logical reason she was experiencing the same erotic dream nightly that outstripped anything she'd ever experienced in real life, why couldn't she figure it out?

Suddenly she caught a flash of red. Pushing away her frustration, she flipped back several pages.

"Fire opals," she said after a moment. Almost reverently, she ran her fingertips across pictures of lush gemstones of various sizes.

"Wow," Claire said, craning her neck to get a good look. "Some of those babies would choke a horse."

"I've heard of fire opals," Allie said.

Thinking about her friend's vast collection of jewelry, Liz gave her a level look. "Is there a gemstone you haven't heard about, Al?"

The heiress arched a blond brow. "Doubtful."

"Find something?"

Sam's voice came from just inches away. Liz glanced across her shoulder where he and Jackson now stood.

"Maybe." She shifted to give them a look at the page. "These are fire opals," she said. "Some are a true red, but the majority have an orangelike cast. But they all have a vein of darker color running through them."

Claire was already digging through the remaining books on the coffee table. "One of these has a section on the history of various gems and myths surrounding them. Here," she said seconds later while hefting a book as thick as a railroad tie from the bottom of the stack.

While she leafed through the pages, Jackson moved beside her and used a forearm to prop up one side of the heavy book.

"Fire opals," Claire read. "Two magical elements are associated with the symbolism of their hot, passionate color: fire and blood."

"Fire and blood," Sam repeated. "The burglar who stole the bracelet said the gem seemed almost alive."

"The pawn shop chick said the stone looked like it had dark veins running through it," Liz added. "Like blood vessels."

"There's more," Claire said, turning a page. "In medieval times, fire opals were considered symbols of the most fervent love between a man and a woman. There's a legend about a bracelet that had a wide gold band twisted to form lovers' knots and a fiery red gem set into its center. It was given to a young woman by the wealthy older man to whom her father betrothed her. The stone had been in the man's family forever, and when he placed it on her wrist, he warned that if she ever removed the bracelet, she would be cursed by her family and the church."

As she continued reading, Claire's voice softened. "Despite the betrothal, the woman had already secretly given her heart to a knight. He swore they would be together, and vowed to win enough in tourney prizes to buy her freedom from the man her father had bound her to."

Liz frowned. The idea of women as chattel to be bartered for lands and property pushed all the wrong buttons with her, although she understood that was how it was done in past centuries.

"The bracelet with the fire opal became associated with tragedy and death when the woman tried to give it to her lover," Claire continued. "That enraged her betrothed, and he wound up killing both her and the knight. Supposedly the spurned lover had some sort of spell cast that would keep the dead lovers apart throughout eternity."

Liz felt her mouth go dry. The legend about the starcrossed lovers sent a tingle of eerie awareness drifting through her.

From behind her, Sam settled a hand on her shoulder. Liz closed her eyes as a whole different kind of tingle coursed from his fingers straight to her belly.

* * *

Liz was still dealing with that erotic sensation a half hour later when she and Sam left the building that housed Claire and Jackson's apartment.

Distance, Liz decided while she locked the door to Home Treasures. The smart thing to do was put space between herself and the man who could rev her engine with a touch.

"You know, Sam, from here it's just as far to my loft as it is to your room at the inn," she said with a sweep of one hand. Under the pale moon, Reunion Square was subdued shades of gray and black, with occasional patches of illumination from the carriage lamps.

"Meaning, you think it'd be a waste of my time to escort you home." Sam's low, quiet words, combined with that smooth Louisiana accent, felt like a velvet glove against her flesh.

Heaven help her. If there was ever a woman who needed to distance herself from pure male temptation, she was it.

"Same thing goes if I were to walk you to the inn. It's a short distance on an unseasonably warm fall night." Despite the tenseness in her shoulders, she managed an idle shrug. "My mental radar isn't picking up on any scuzzballs in the vicinity. So, I see no reason we can't both save time and go our separate ways from here."

She started to turn away, then stopped, stared down at the hand he'd shot out to grip her elbow. "There a problem, Broussard?"

"I know a reason. My Grandmother Broussard would have a piece of my hide if she found out I failed to escort my dinner companion home."

"If you don't tell her, I sure won't."

"She'd know." His fingers tightened on Liz's elbow as they moved along the sidewalk where carriage lamps placed at precise distances cast pools of security. "Grandmother has this sort of built-in ESP."

Resigned that she wasn't going to shake him loose, Liz slid him an upward glance and smiled. "Your granny sounds like a cool woman."

"She is. And full of surprises. I never know what I'll find when I show up at her house."

"Like what?"

"The steps up to her porch might be covered with red brick dust."

"Why?"

"The dust wards off evil spirits."

Liz pursed her mouth. "Does it work?"

"Must. I've never spotted an evil spirit in her house," Sam returned mildly.

Thinking of Dream Lover with a gun, Liz wondered if she ought to give red brick dust a try. "What other stuff has your granny surprised you with?"

"If I open her freezer during a certain phase of the moon, it's a sure bet I'll find scraps of paper with names written on them. That's grandmother's way of taking care of destructive people."

"We should try that with bad guys," Liz commented as they approached the landscaped area that led to The Montgomery. "It'd be a lot cheaper than tossing them in jail."

Around them, small spotlights spread fans of light across flower beds ablaze with mums and pansies blooming with fall colors. Beyond the beds, additional lights illuminated the facade of the ten-story high-rise.

Liz paused beside an ivy-covered arbor that housed a teakwood bench. "So, do your conjure women aunts and cousins also do the kinds of stuff your granny does?"

"Pretty much. Maybe since I grew up around all that is the reason I spotted something today that might be related to our case. I don't think it's hit you yet."

"What?" Liz asked, her spine stiffening at the prospect she'd missed some looming clue.

"The similarity between the gold bracelet and your birthmark."

She furrowed her forehead. "There's no similarity."

"It's the same way with anything you see every day. After a while you don't really *see* it." As he spoke, Sam slid his hand from her elbow to her wrist and nudged up the cuff of her black leather jacket. "It first hit me when you showed Temple's sketch of the bracelet to the pawn shop owner. Then tonight, when Claire read the description from the book, it said the gold cuff was twisted to form lovers' knots. The mark on your wrist could be described that way, too."

Feeling a mix of confusion and surprise, Liz tugged her arm from his hold. She angled her wrist toward the nearest light and studied her birthmark.

"Let me get this straight," she said after a moment. "You believe my birthmark matches a bracelet worn in medieval times by a woman murdered by some rich guy she spurned?"

"There are so many unexplainable things going on with this case that I don't know what I believe," Sam said levelly.

Liz slowly lowered her arm. Although she wanted to deny the similarity, she couldn't. Sam was right. For an instant, her mind struggled to find a sensible explanation. But there wasn't one. She was beginning to feel as if she'd fallen down a rabbit hole into a strange and unpredictable parallel world.

"Do you believe in coincidence, Broussard?"

He leaned a shoulder against the arbor. In the dim wash of light, the combination of dark hair and smoke-colored eyes made him look unbearably sexy. "I never have before."

"Do you now?"

"No."

"Neither do I. So, there has to be a logical explanation for why I've got a birthmark that bears a resemblance to an old bracelet that's got a curse hanging over it." For emphasis, Liz began ticking off the items on her fingers.

"And why a man who had a reproduction of that bracelet omitted it from the list of property stolen from his home. Which wouldn't matter if he hadn't also owned the gun that killed the victim of a thirty-year-old murder we're investigating."

"Don't forget that the same man writes books on English medieval law. And we just heard one heck of a legend from medieval times."

Liz flung up a hand in frustration. "So, how the heck are we supposed to make sense of all that?"

Sam reached out, caught a lock of her hair and toyed with it gently. "Good question."

With his hand so near to her face, Liz's throat tightened. She wasn't sure what would happen if he touched her.

Just the prospect that he might sent heat creeping up the back of her neck. "Well, we aren't going to get anything figured out tonight, so thanks for walking me home. Your gentlemanly ways have kept you safe from your granny's wrath."

Slowly he twined her hair around his fingers. "There is one thing I can make sense of," he said, ignoring her blatant attempt at dismissal.

His hand was so close to her cheek, Liz could feel the heat from his skin. "What?"

"It's getting harder to keep my hands off of you. In fact, I don't *want* to keep my hands off of you."

Inside she went very still, knowing she was fighting the same battle. Even so, she might have denied it but she had a hunch he could see the truth in her eyes.

She wet her lips and said the only thing she could think of. "We're partners."

His hands slid beneath her hair and slowly folded around her nape. His palms were warm and heavy against her skin. She could feel the strength in him but sensed the control. The combination was electrifying.

His thumbs moved gently just behind her ears. He eased her head back slightly and lowered his mouth to within a whisper of hers.

"Partners, who are off duty," he said. "And standing in this arbor, where no one can see us."

"We still have to work together. For a while, anyway." She was surprised her voice didn't tremble in unison with her legs. "Until this case is over."

"Liz?"

"Yes?"

"Shut up."

His lips grazed hers. Her eyes fluttered shut. "Okay."

The kiss was a real one this time, not the chaste brush of the lips they'd shared in the microfilm room. And it was exactly what she had suspected it would be.

Devastating.

Excitement sparked along every nerve ending. Flames erupted beneath her flesh, fierce and intense. A liquid heat welled somewhere in the region below her belly. She was aware of the frenzied pounding of her own heart.

Pulling her closer, Sam deepened the kiss with slow deliberation.

Her fingers dived into his hair and fisted there. His mouth was so tempting, his taste so enticing. She could feel the unmistakable pressure of his arousal against her thigh.

His mouth slanted across hers. He drew his palms down her throat, slid his fingers inside her leather jacket and covered her breasts. A sense of urgency pulsed through her.

That he made no effort to conceal his hunger played havoc with the last shreds of her common sense.

Just a kiss, she thought. How much damage could one—or a few—kisses do? Even between partners.

"I've been thinking how it would be to kiss you again," Sam breathed against her throat. "Really kiss you. I was going crazy waiting to find out."

She'd been going crazy herself. In fact, her life could be described as not-so-sane these days.

One of his hands tunneled through her hair. The other moved over the curve of her hip. She felt his fingers slide beneath the hem of her sweater. It suddenly hit her that over the past weeks, she'd been touched by her then-fiancé, a dreamed-up hunk and a sexy Louisiana cop.

But Sam Broussard's kiss was nothing like Andrew's soft, gentle ones. Sam's was raw. Primitive. And, heaven help her, the feel of his mouth, the scrape of his stubbled jaw was such a close match to Dream Lover's that Liz felt the immediate intimacy of long-time lovers. A moan slid up her throat as she struggled with the dizzying knowledge that she truly had stumbled into some strange, twin universe.

That, or she was a shoe-in for the loony bin. And if she didn't put on the brakes now, she was afraid her entire life would crash and burn.

With his hand still wrapped in her hair Sam dragged her head back. He gazed down at her, his eyes gleaming. "Why don't you invite me up to your loft?"

His voice was low and husky and had her swallowing hard. She didn't just want to ask him upstairs, she wanted to *drag* him there. But she couldn't. Didn't dare.

"We're moving too fast." She tried with little success to catch her breath. Every pulse point in her body felt like a jackhammer.

When he made no move to release her, she jerked back. And felt the slide of his fingers against her flesh as his hand eased from beneath her sweater.

Her heart and lungs were straining. She had no control over them. No control over the ache of wanting him that was so huge it left little room for reason. That knowledge shot a dazed fear into her system. It wasn't right that one man should be able to do this to her.

"I don't know how long you've been divorced." Her voice—her entire body—quaked. "But it was just a couple of weeks ago that I was set to marry Andrew." Desperate to regain some sense of control, she curled her fingers into her palms until her nails bit into her flesh. "I still don't know why I couldn't go through with it. Twice. That's a lot of baggage to haul around. I need time—"

"I'm not divorced."

For a moment she just stared up at Sam. It wasn't just his words that caught her off guard, but his voice had gone from thick and husky to hard and raw.

"You…said you'd been married, that it didn't work out."

"She died."

"Oh." Liz shook her head. "I'm sorry. I—"

"You're not the only one with baggage." His eyes were intense, unwavering. "My wife didn't just die. I killed her."

Chapter 8

I killed my wife.

"Guess that put a damper on the mood," Sam said as he stared down into Liz's shocked face.

Because sharp, strong desire continued to surge through him, he dragged his attention away from the rapid pulse still throbbing at the base of her throat. Every muscle in his body was tight. The hunger clawing at him was invasive, blinding. But it was more than just lust.

Stronger than lust.

The knowledge that what he felt for her was beyond a feral hunger terrified him right down to his marrow. And it was dangerous as hell, because whatever the emotion was ripping at his insides, it had lowered his guard enough that he'd blurted the truth about Tanya.

He sure as hell hadn't intended to say that, but it was probably best he had. By doing so, he'd put the skids on any chance of his and Liz getting closer. Intimate. There would be no placing her at risk by repeating the mistakes he'd made with Tanya.

And working with Liz was now probably out of the question. How willing would she be to continue partnering with a man who'd gotten his own wife killed?

"I should go," he said and turned.

"The hell with that." Liz stepped in front of him so fast he had to jerk back to keep from plowing into her. Gone was the stunned look in her eyes. Now, they were shimmering green. *Hot* green.

"You don't kiss me blind, then drop a bomb like that and just stroll away."

"My *strolling away* is for your own damn good." The words ground between his teeth as he turned away from her and stared off into the night. Around them, Reunion Square was a landscape of shadows and pale moonlight. Faintly he could hear the music and chatter from the small pub on the square's opposite side.

And the hammering of his own heart.

He scrubbed a hand over his face. His gut tightened just thinking about the feel of Liz's sleek, lush body pressed against him. He had responded to her as if he were dying of thirst and she was the well. A well he had drunk from before, during a time in the past he had no memory of. Why the hell was the feel of her, the taste of her, all so damn familiar?

"So you think your walking away is for my own

good," she said. "And it's somehow connected to your wife's death?"

"Not somehow. It *is* connected."

In his peripheral vision, he watched Liz settle on the bench beneath the arbor. "Don't you think you ought to explain?"

He hadn't talked about Tanya since she died, not to anyone. Just the thought of doing that now sent the bitterness that had lodged deep inside him since that nightmare day swirling into his throat. But he'd opened the door by bringing up Tanya and he owed Liz an explanation.

He sat beside her, leaned his elbows on his knees and swept his gaze across the flower beds. Beneath the soft illumination from landscape lighting, the orange and yellow blooms shimmered like ghosts.

Barely breathing, Liz studied Sam while he stared off into the distance. His profile was tough, contained. Grim. A muscle ticked in his jaw, his lips were compressed as if he found nothing joyous in his life. She suspected that was the case, considering what was in his past. But she didn't for one minute believe he'd killed his wife, not in the literal sense. Otherwise, he wouldn't be walking around free, much less wearing a badge.

"It's complicated," he said finally. "I'm not sure where to start."

"The beginning," she suggested softly. "How did you meet?"

"I saw her standing on the side of the road, glaring

at the flat tire on her car. I pulled over, showed her my badge and offered to help."

"What was her name?"

"Tanya. She was the hostess at an upscale country-western bar. To thank me for changing the tire, she offered to buy me a drink. We hit it off, big time. Got married a month later."

Liz blinked. "That was fast."

"Way too fast." He swiped a hand over the back of his neck. "At first, she thought my job was sexy. She didn't feel that way when she had to deal with my being a cop on a daily basis."

"She worried about you," Liz guessed. She'd gone through the same thing with Andrew.

"That's what I thought at first. Turned out that wasn't it. I worked days and took night classes to finish up my criminal justice degree. It was all the hours I was gone that Tanya didn't like. I told her to be patient, that I would graduate in a couple of months, then transfer to the night shift. We'd have our days free then."

To Liz, that sounded like a short sacrifice with a pot of gold at the end. From the edge that had settled in Sam's voice, she suspected Tanya hadn't wanted to wait.

"Then I got assigned to a multiagency task force and that pretty much sucked up any free time I had. Tanya accused me of loving the job more than her."

"Did you?" Liz couldn't help but ask.

"No." He straightened beside her on the bench, raked a hand through his dark hair. "The job was im-

portant to me, but I was crazy about her. I thought…."
His eyes narrowed. "Doesn't matter now what I
thought. When you get orders to work a special assignment, there's not much you can do about the hours."

"There isn't," Liz agreed. "I've watched other cops
try to juggle the demands of work and family. There
never seems to be an equal balance."

"Sure wasn't for Tanya and me. I wasn't around, so
she had an affair."

Liz heard the splinter of pain that worked its way
into his voice. She felt a rush of sympathy, but quelled
it. Instinct told her that was the last thing Sam Broussard wanted from her.

"That had to have hurt," she said quietly.

"Like hell." He fisted a hand against the bench's arm.
"She was sleeping with her new boss at the bar. When
I confronted her about the affair, she tossed into my face
how selfish I was, that I was already a cop and didn't
need a degree to do my job. If I loved her, I would ask
for a transfer off the task force, drop out of college and
work the night shift so we could be together during the
day. That maybe if I paid attention to *her* needs she
wouldn't have had to look elsewhere for companion-
ship."

There's a low blow, Liz thought. Tanya had certainly done an ace job at lobbing the ball back over the
net and hitting her husband with all the blame.

Sam's fist now drummed against the bench's arm.
"I left home and stayed drunk for a couple of days.
When I sobered up, I thought maybe she was right—

when I wasn't on duty I was in class. Or studying. Maybe if I'd been around more often, more attentive, she wouldn't have gotten involved with another man. So, I went back home, quit college and transferred to the night shift."

"Did that help?"

"No. Despite her promise to end her affair, she didn't even make the effort to come straight home after work. When I asked her to find a new job, she refused. It only took a few days for me to find proof she was still fooling around with her boss."

Good old Tanya. As far as Liz could tell, the only thing Sam had been guilty of so far was working long hours.

"Did you confront her again?"

"No, I was too pissed off. I decided to wait until I cooled down."

Smart, Liz thought. Given the circumstances, not many men would possess that amount of self-control.

"A couple of hours after I found out the affair was still going on, Tanya called on my cell. I was working a crime scene at the time. She said she was late getting off work, and could I go by the grocery store on my way home and pick up some things? It all hit me then, the fury and frustration. So I told her I was busy, that *my* work sometimes *had* to come first, and at least I was *at work* and not off screwing my boss. I hung up on her. I knew then that I didn't even want to try to save the marriage.

"I turned off my cell and blocked out everything except the scene I was working. About an hour later, my lieutenant showed up. He told me Tanya had walked in on an armed robbery in progress at a grocery store."

Liz closed her eyes. Somehow, someway, she knew what was coming, and her heart bled for Sam.

"He told me the robber had shot and killed her. I *insisted* on going to the store. I stood there, staring at my wife lying in a pool of blood, knowing that if I'd agreed to stop and buy some damn milk on my way home that she would have still been alive."

"Maybe," Liz said carefully. She had worked in Homicide for several years and had witnessed death up close and personal. But never as personal as this. "Maybe not. That's something you won't ever know for sure."

"What I *know* is, I made a lousy husband. I couldn't keep my wife faithful. Couldn't protect her."

He turned his head, met Liz's gaze. "Ironic, don't you think, that everything inside me tells me I need to protect you? I'm the last guy who ought to be taking on the job."

The bleakness in his eyes was raw. Raw and deep and laced with despair that Liz never could have suspected was lurking inside the controlled Louisiana cop who'd shown up in her office less than a week ago.

"I think there are a lot of ironic things going on with us," she said. "Things that we may never figure out. But I do know one thing for sure."

"What?"

"You didn't kill your wife, Sam. Logically you probably know that."

"Yeah, I'm not the guy who pulled the trigger, I've *got* that. But logic doesn't help when I close my eyes and see her body in a pool of blood. And I know, without a doubt, she wouldn't have wound up there if it wasn't for me."

Liz said nothing. How could she debate that when he was probably right?

He matched her gaze for a long moment. "You're the first person I've talked to about her. I thought it would be like touching a wound, keeping it fresh and bleeding." He shook his head. "Telling you was easier than I thought."

"I'm glad you told me." She paused for a moment. "How long ago did this happen?"

"She's been dead two and a half years."

Liz closed her eyes against a rush of sadness and sympathy. That was a long time to carry around so much guilt.

"Does your wife's death have something to do with why your lieutenant ordered you to take leave time?"

"The only thing that kept thoughts of her at bay was the job. So, I worked. Went in on my days off. Volunteered for overtime." Sam shook his head. "Looking back, I can see I was on automatic pilot most of the time. I went through the motions of being a cop, but I put nothing of myself into my cases."

He shifted on the bench. "That changed when I recovered the Colt during the bust at the sting operation. The instant I touched the gun I felt something, some spark. For the first time since Tanya's murder I felt the fire-in-the-belly for the job."

"So, that's why you wanted to work on this case," Liz said quietly.

"That's one reason. You're another. There's something there, Liz. I felt it the first time I saw you rushing toward me in the basement hallway."

"I felt something, too, Sam." Because she ached for him, she lifted a hand to his cheek. "You know, don't you, that between us, we're hauling around enough baggage to keep a skycap busy full-time?"

His mouth hitched on one side. "Good way to look at it."

"We don't have any business getting involved." And because she felt a tiny surge of panic over the thought of never being in his arms again, she added, "At least until we each get some past things resolved."

"At least." His gaze swept across her face. "No matter the past, being here, working with you is the right thing to do. For me, it feels right."

"For me, too." Lowering her hand, she curled her fingers into her palm as if to hold his essence close. "So, how about we agree to table everything else for the time being and focus on the Windsor case?"

"Agreed." Keeping his gaze locked with hers, Sam skimmed his palm down the length of her hair. "For now."

Sam's cell phone rang twenty minutes later, just as he unlocked the door to his room at the Reunion Square Inn.

He checked the display and winced when he saw the

caller was his Grandmother Broussard. She disliked making phone calls. *Never* made them unless something was of vital importance.

The woman had been as tenacious as his lieutenant about him taking time off. Which was why Sam had put off calling her after he signed on to the Windsor investigation.

"Grandmother, how are you?" he asked while shrugging out of his leather bomber jacket.

"I am well, Samuel. Rested. Too bad we can't say the same thing about you."

"I'm sleeping fine."

"Not in Colorado."

Scowling, Sam lowered himself onto the edge of the bed. "You've been talking to Frank." He was going to kill his partner.

"He paid me a visit this evening. While he ate a bowl of my homemade spoon bread, I asked if you had called to let him know how you're enjoying his family's cabin in Colorado. He said you weren't there."

"I'm not. After I heard details of the homicide the gun I recovered connects to, I decided to stay in Oklahoma City for a while. I imagine Frank told you that."

"He did. Samuel, I'm worried about you."

He pictured his grandmother sitting on the couch in the small, cozy house he'd bought her. As always, her dark eyes were alert and bright in her sharp-featured face, her long white hair piled haphazardly on top of her head.

Sam didn't like knowing she spent time worrying about him.

"I'm fine." He shoved a hand through his hair. "If I'd gone to Colorado, the homicide case would have stayed in my head. So I wouldn't have gotten much rest there."

"The case holds personal importance for you."

The sureness in her tone had Sam hesitating. When it came to ferreting out information, his grandmother was as skilled as any seasoned police interrogator. Then there was her uncanny talent for reading people.

Like Tanya.

When he'd introduced the two women, his grandmother had taken him aside and pronounced that his fiancée wasn't the right woman for him. That she would bring him misery.

Back then, he'd been unwilling to let his grandmother's innate sixth sense divine his future. So he'd refused to give credence to her portending of doom.

He had always been grateful she had never once said I told you so.

"There's something about the old homicide that gets to me," he said carefully. "The police officer working the case got permission for me to consult."

Sam heard the shuffle of cards come across the line. Resigned, he propped his spine against the bank of pillows lining the headboard. His grandmother was big on tarot-card readings.

"This police officer is a woman?"

Sam narrowed his eyes. "What card did you just turn over?"

"The Lovers. It's a card of emotions, Samuel."

"So you've told me." No doubt about it, after kissing Liz, his emotions were churning.

The jangle of the silver bracelets his grandmother wore practically up to her elbows told Sam she'd dealt another card.

"The Tower," she said. "It has an energy similar to death in that it's both a destructive and a creative force."

"I *am* working a homicide," Sam reminded her.

Her bracelets clacked again. Then came a humming silence.

"Grandmother, what's the next card?"

"The Knight of Swords. Samuel, when results are not achieved, the knight will try to resolve things his way."

"Which is?"

"Through violence."

Sam's gut tightened. He remembered the murky image that had swum into his mind of a young woman fleeing from a dark-haired man with a bloody sword.

"I don't suppose you know this knight's name?"

"If I did, I would write it down and put it in my freezer. That would take care of him." His grandmother sighed. "Samuel, you're where you are for a reason. The cards tell me you must be careful, not only with your heart but your life."

"I will," he assured her quietly. Not only would he take care with his own life, but with Liz's, too.

Late Friday afternoon, Liz looked up from the file on her desk when the bullnecked civilian employee assigned to the mail room stuck his head into the cold case office. "There a Detective Broussard here?"

"You got him."

Liz watched Sam rise from the table that served as his makeshift work area. He wore black cords and a gunmetal-gray shirt that matched his eyes. His dark hair was rumpled from finger combing and a day's worth of stubble darkened his jaw. When he reached for the mailing envelope, her gaze went to his long-fingered hand. Just the memory of his touch made all her juices flow and her breasts tighten.

Three days had passed since they stood in the alcove outside of The Montgomery and he'd kissed her senseless. Three days since they agreed to focus solely on the Windsor investigation.

Three days of hell, working so closely that Liz could *smell* him. No cologne. Not even the smell of soap. Just a compelling scent that was so uniquely Sam's that it set her off like a California brushfire.

Still, they'd made that agreement for a reason and she intended to stick to it. She was not a child with her face pressed up to the candy store window. She didn't let herself have everything she wanted.

But, holy heaven, did the man know how to kiss!

The mailroom clerk disappeared down the hallway while Sam checked the return address on the mailer. "Max Hogan's military records," Sam said, referring to the marine who died with Geneviève Windsor.

The phone on Liz's desk rang just as Sam settled back in his chair. She swept up the receiver and answered.

The caller was David York's secretary. She asked Liz to hold for the judge.

"No problem." Liz tilted back in her chair, the phone tucked under her ear while she watched Sam pull a thick stack of paper out of the mailer.

"Sergeant Scott?"

"Yes, Judge," Liz replied, and saw the way Sam's face hardened at the mention of York's name. For whatever reason, her partner's instincts apparently were still blasting the message she needed some sort of protection from the judge.

"You requested that I search my records for the name of the construction company that did the work at my home thirty years ago."

"That's right." Liz straightened in her chair. Having the name of that company might lead her and Sam to the workers who had access to the desk from which the judge's Colt had been stolen, and later used to kill Geneviève Windsor.

"Did you find the information?" Liz asked while reaching for a notepad and pen.

"Unfortunately, no. I purge my personal files every few years, so I imagine I simply shredded those documents long ago."

"Thanks for looking." Liz scowled. While working in Homicide, she had learned that possessing an insatiable curiosity, even to the point of nosiness or snoopiness, came in handy. A person just never knew what information might turn into the glue that connected all the pieces.

"Judge, exactly what work did you have done on your house?"

"Let's see…" York's voice drifted off as if he were mulling over the question. "I had an addition built onto my garage," he said after a moment. "And some renovation done to my kitchen. There were a few other cosmetic changes made to various rooms, but after all this time I don't remember what they were."

"Understandable. I appreciate you looking for the information."

Liz's thoughts switched to the gold bracelet with the fire opal that J. D. Temple claimed to have stolen from York's house. Rolling her hand over, she gazed at the birthmark on the inside of her wrist which apparently resembled the same type of lovers' knots that formed the bracelet's cuff.

Liz was tempted to ask York if he had owned the bracelet and, if so, why he hadn't reported it stolen. But another thing she'd learned while working in Homicide was not to ask certain questions until she knew the answer, or at least had some idea of what it might be. Besides, at this point there was nothing linking the bracelet to her current case.

"I'm looking forward to seeing you Monday night at the reception."

York's comment pulled her thoughts back.

"Monday night," she repeated, and plucked the invitation he'd delivered from the organizer on one corner of her desk. Although the Committee of One Hundred had put muscle behind getting the federal grant that funded the cold case office, Liz disliked formal gatherings so much she would have begged off from going. But the memo she'd received from the chief ordering her to go as the department's representative had nixed her getting out of attending.

After telling York she'd see him there, Liz ended the call.

Sam glanced up from Hogan's military records. "Sounds like York didn't come through with the name of the construction company."

"Right." Liz turned her pen end over end while she considered what York had said. "There might be a way to find out anyway."

"How?"

"He said he had an addition built onto his garage. Remember the picture of York's house that I showed Temple when we interviewed him at the prison?"

"Yes."

"When I took the picture, I noticed that York's garage is a separate structure. It's connected to the house by a covered walkway." Liz opened a drawer and retrieved her phone directory for city departments. "I don't know what the law was thirty years ago, but the present city ordinance requires any contractor adding an addition to an existing structure to apply for a building permit. And to display that permit at the work site."

"Is the contractor's name on the permit?"

"I don't think so. But if the law was the same back then, and if Public Works has past building permits computerized, they should be able to do a search by the location where the work was performed."

"And what construction company applied for the permit." Sam angled his chin. "Good thinking."

"Hold off on the kudos until I find out if that information is even available." She began leafing through the phone directory. "Find anything interesting in Hogan's file?"

"Not yet," Sam replied. "His firearms qualifications show he was an excellent shot. There's no mention of any disciplinary problems. No record of any violent behavior or problem with women."

"I haven't been able to find anyone who knew him," Liz said while punching numbers into her phone. "I've left a message for a woman who worked with Geneviève Windsor at the oil company to call me. I'm hoping Geneviève talked to her about—"

Liz broke off when the call she'd placed to the Public Works department was answered. Ten minutes later, she had the name of the company that had been issued a building permit thirty years ago to build the addition to York's garage.

Her hope that her luck would hold out faded when her call to P. R. Usher & Son Construction went to voice mail. She left her name and cell number. It was just after five o'clock on Friday, and half the people in the city were probably headed to happy hour. Her message no doubt wouldn't be returned until Monday.

Thoughts of the weekend had her easing out a breath. She'd debated all day about whether or not to ask Sam if he had plans. Considering that her insides went into nuclear meltdown whenever he got close, she would probably be smart not to even bring up the subject. But he was a stranger in town and the thought of leaving him to fend for himself tugged at her conscience.

And, damn, could the man kiss. Which made no difference at all since what she had in mind involved hundreds of people. *Safety in numbers,* she assured herself.

She opened her mouth to ask him about his plans, but hesitated when she saw the rigid set of his shoulders. She was so attuned to him now, she knew he'd picked up on something in the marine's file.

"What did you find?"

"Maybe nothing." Sam looked up, his eyes somber. "I'm not sure it means a damn thing."

She moved to stand beside his work table and glanced down at Hogan's file. "That what means a damn thing?"

"Hogan was assigned to Force Recon, the Marine equivalent of Navy SEALS. That was followed by two combat tours and a stint as an embassy guard."

"Does his military experience tie in some way to Windsor's murder?"

"No." Leaning back in his chair, Sam ran a finger along his stubbled jaw. "At least not that I can tell."

"Then what?"

"We've got another damn coincidence to add to our already long list." He gestured toward the file.

"Hogan's service in the corps is almost identical to mine."

"Identical?"

"On paper, the guy looks like me."

Liz frowned. There were so many—*too many*—weird things going on with their investigation. "Was Hogan also from Louisiana?"

"No, California. But his parents are listed as deceased, and his sole relative was his grandmother. All of which we can probably write off as one of those serendipitous things."

"Doesn't look like we have a choice."

"No." Sam closed the cover on the file. "Any luck tracking down the construction company that did the work at York's house?"

Liz realized he'd been so immersed in Hogan's record that he'd paid scant attention to what she'd been doing.

"The good news is that the construction company is still in business. The bad news is that everyone's gone for the weekend."

She slid her tongue over her lips. "Speaking of the weekend, I was wondering if you have plans?"

Leaning back in his chair, Sam stretched out his long legs. "I was thinking about going to the Murrah bombing memorial. The desk clerk said it's a short walk from the inn."

"It is, and you should wait until dusk to go. Seeing the Field of Empty Chairs, with all 168 of them illuminated, grabs you by the throat."

"All right." Sam cocked his head. "Any particular reason you asked about my plans?"

She jammed her hands into the pockets of her slacks. "You know how your grandmother would have skinned you alive for not walking me home the other night?"

"Yeah."

"You're not the only one with manners. I don't like the idea of my temporary partner sitting alone over the weekend."

"That's neighborly of you, Liz. What do you have in mind?"

"Tomorrow, the Reunion Square Association is sponsoring its annual Fall Festival," she answered. "There'll be booths set up in the square selling food, crafts and an assortment of other things. Allie, Claire and I are manning a booth. So, if you're out, you might want to drop by."

"Maybe I will. What booth?"

"Face painting. It's almost Halloween, so the kids wear their costumes and we paint some little something on their cheek that goes with whatever they're dressed up as."

"You any good with a paintbrush?" The warmth in his voice was unmistakable, and made Liz's skin feel hot and tight.

"Visit our booth and I'll show you."

"I don't want my face painted." He pursed his mouth. "How about you paint me a temporary tattoo instead?"

She kept her gaze locked on his. "Depends on where you want it."

His smile was slow and just a little wicked and she had to repress the instinctive urge to take a step back. Or maybe forward.

"I'll put some thought into that and let you know."

Chapter 9

The following afternoon, Sam walked through Reunion Square, amazed at its transformation. Lining the outer perimeter of the grassy area were booths and tables sporting an array of handicrafts, baked goods and potted mums that formed oceans of blooming color. On a nearby table, a row of pumpkins carved with an artist's expertise smiled out at the milling suburban crowd.

Leaves from the soaring oaks dotting the square had piled onto the grass, the red, yellow and partial green giving the event a New England effect. Their crisp smell mixed with the delicious scent of hot apple cider.

Sam stopped and bought a cup from a teenage girl with a dusting of freckles across her nose. "Where's the face painting?" he asked while accepting his change.

He thanked the teen, then headed in the direction she pointed.

When he spotted the booth where Liz told him she would be working with Allie and Claire, he didn't approach it. Instead he stood off to one side of a table where two women were selling cornstalk dolls dressed in yellow gingham.

Sipping the hot cider, he surveilled the booth's operation. It didn't take long for it to become apparent that Allie and Claire were the artists in residence while Liz took money and made change.

His gaze tracked her as she rode herd on a handful of Halloween-costumed children waiting in line. Over her trim, well-worn jeans and dark sweater she wore a black chef's apron, spattered with various colors of paint. Instead of the usual braid, her coppery hair was bunched through a black baseball cap in a long curly ponytail. Sam arched a brow when he spotted the eye-popping-yellow paint on the ponytail's tip.

Despite their banter yesterday about tattoos, he hadn't been certain he would show up today. Telling her about Tanya, then hearing Liz's soft words and seeing the understanding in her eyes had ripped something inside him.

It had been a very long time since he'd had anyone to talk to like that. A long time since he'd felt a woman's sweet touch against his cheek. He'd forgotten about those things. Forgotten how much comfort a woman could give a man. How much she could make him feel whole.

Still, he had no intention of putting Liz at risk by screwing up with her the way he'd done with his dead wife. So, he'd convinced himself he had the self-control to fight whatever the hell it was that seemed to stretch and grow between them.

Dammit, he didn't want to worry about her. Didn't want to have to think about her at all, but a capricious, malicious fate had decreed otherwise. Which was why he was standing here, watching her try to reason with a sulky-faced kid dressed like an Old West lawman.

At one point, her chin took on the same stubborn slope as the kid's, and Sam found himself fighting a smile. Seconds later, his eyes narrowed when he saw the shadows of weariness under her eyes. Concern tightened his gut.

Hell, he thought, if he was going to stew over her losing a little sleep, he might as well stop fighting it. Whatever was between them was deep and strong and powerful.

Crumpling his empty cup, he tossed it into a trash barrel and made his way toward the booth.

"Take my word for it, Timmy," Liz said through gritted teeth while leaning over the kid with a gun belt wrapped around his skinny hips. "Getting something painted on your cheek isn't sissy."

"Is, too!"

"Is, not." Liz sucked in a breath and rubbed at the headache that ground in the center of her forehead.

She hadn't slept a wink after Dream Lover showed

up this morning at the stroke of two. The cold-blooded terror she'd felt when he brandished the gun had jolted her awake, leaving her pulse pounding and her flesh icy cold.

When her system calmed and fear no longer burned her throat, she'd lain in the dark, struggling in vain to remember more of the strange words he growled with such urgency. And wondering how the kiss and taste of the lover her subconscious had created could be so much like her flesh-and-blood temporary partner's. Or was it just wishful thinking on her part? With all that churning inside her, there'd been no shutting off her mind and falling back to sleep.

So, she'd shown up at the face painting booth with fatigue falling over her like a fog. All day she'd dealt with children in dire need of a nap and her patience had frayed like an overused rope. *This,* she thought as she stared down at the miniature Wyatt Earp, was why she would walk barefoot on hot coals before agreeing to an assignment in the juvie division.

Reaching out, she nudged the one-size-too-big cowboy hat back far enough so she could see the storm clouds in Timmy's eyes. "Look, just because your sister got a fairy painted on her cheek doesn't mean you have to get the same thing. Your mom has already bought you a ticket, so give us all a break and at least look at the pictures we've got. Maybe you'll like something you see."

"I already looked, 'n they're all sissy! I'm a *sheriff*, not a sissy!"

"How about a badge, Sheriff?"

Liz jolted at the sound of Sam's voice coming from right behind her. And then the instant buzz of reaction to his presence shot through her.

She shifted to face him. The crisp breeze ruffled his dark hair, his jaw was stubbled, and he wore aviator sunglasses that reflected her image back at her. The man looked so totally sexy she wanted to slide her hands beneath his leather bomber jacket and snuggle close.

Instead she crammed her fists into the pockets of her paint-spattered apron. It might be easier to think of Broussard solely as her temporary partner if she didn't feel as if she were going to go up like a bottle rocket every time he so much as looked her way.

"A badge?" Timmy asked hopefully.

Before she could even wrap her mind around a reply, Sam had crouched, putting himself and the kid eye to eye.

"You're the law around here, right?" he asked, slicking a fingertip over the plastic badge pinned to the boy's plaid shirt.

"I'm the sheriff. I arrest bad guys."

"Well, Sheriff, it seems to me if you got a badge painted on your cheek, the bad guys would know how tough you really are."

"They would?"

"You bet. I'm a lawman, too. Trust me on this." Sam shifted, his expression as serious as stone as he retrieved a leather case out of the back pocket of his jeans. Flipping open the cover, he gave Timmy a close-up look at his gold detective's badge. While Sam continued speaking in quiet tones, the boy's face brightened like the sun.

Liz gave a despairing shove at her hair. She was too exhausted, too emotionally drained to fight off the wave of feelings that assaulted her on seeing big, tough Sam Broussard coaxing a face-splitting grin onto a little boy's face.

Wearily she closed her eyes. And in that unguarded instant, she fell all the way in love.

Which wasn't a pleasant thing. It wasn't the flowers, soft music and floating hearts she'd felt with Andrew. No, this was a fast, hard plunge into love with a man she hardly knew. The landing was rocky, with a myriad of problems at the bottom.

Her breathing shallowed as a mix of emotions swirled around her. She had no idea how to even begin to deal with this.

"All right!" Literally bouncing in his cowboy boots, Timmy tugged on her apron. "I want a badge!"

Liz gave herself a mental shake and tried to look unruffled.

"Good idea, Sheriff," she said while Sam rose beside her to his full height. "Go tell Miss Allie what you want. She'll fix you right up."

"Cool!"

While Timmy scampered off, Liz tilted her head back so she could see Sam's face past the rim of her baseball cap. "You're good, Broussard."

One of his shoulders lifted. "My cousins have kids.

They all get sulky at one time or another. Dealing with them just takes patience."

"I ran out of that when some idiot kid dressed like a big yellow sponge dipped the ends of my hair into the paint jar."

Sam arched a dark brow. "Did you take him down?"

"Believe me, I was tempted." Pursing her mouth, she studied Sam. It was late afternoon, and like a schoolgirl with a crush she'd watched for him to show up most of the day. Which was something she'd barely admitted to herself much less to Allie and Claire.

"So did you drop by to get that temporary tattoo?"

"No, I came to get you."

"*Get* me?"

"*Hoping* to get you," he amended. "Will you have dinner with me when you get done here?"

Liz felt a lump form in her throat. Everything had happened so fast between them she could barely think. She was trying to be smart. Trying to slow things down, to hold on to a modicum of control. "We agreed to keep things between us strictly business."

"I remember." The mirrored sunglasses kept her from seeing his eyes, but she felt the intensity of his gaze on her face. "I've thought about what we agreed to, and I suggest a compromise."

Liz glanced across her shoulder to make sure Claire and Allie had things in the booth under control. They did.

"I'm listening. What compromise?"

"You've been a cop a while, so you've probably had your share of partners."

"Right. So?"

"How many of them have you hashed out the details of a case with over drinks or dinner?"

"I've done that with every partner I've had since I made detective."

"Same goes for me," Sam said. "It helps to get away from the station and talk things out in different surroundings. Sometimes a change of scene helps you come up with a new lead. Do you know of any reason the same thing shouldn't apply to us?"

Only that she'd never before had the hots for one of her partners.

Liz shoved her hands deeper into her apron's pockets. "So, you're suggesting that whenever we're together, we deal only with the Windsor investigation? Whether we're on or off duty?"

"You're a quick study, Sergeant Scott."

"Millions concur," she murmured, and felt her pulse skip when he took a step closer.

He lowered his voice so only she could hear. "I'm losing ground here, Liz. I'm losing it fast. There's something about you that grabbed hold of me the minute I saw you. I've tried to shake it, but I can't. I care about you, and I want to spend time with you. On duty and off."

"Sam." Her heart was pounding like a jackhammer. "You're not the only one who's lost ground. Dammit."

He leaned in. "Dammit?" His accent wrapped around her like smoke.

"We have a case to solve." The lump in her throat had tightened into a knot and she could barely get the words out. "I don't think we're going to do that unless we keep what's between us under control."

"I'm not arguing that." He slid off his sunglasses, hooked one earpiece into the pocket of his shirt. All the while, his flint-gray eyes stayed locked on hers. "We've both worn a badge long enough to know it's possible to function as a cop when there are things going on in our personal lives. We've already agreed to cool things until we each deal with what's in our past. That doesn't change."

Glancing away, Liz was surprised to feel the sting of tears. She'd never expected to experience love so soon after splitting with Andrew, but the feeling was there, big and bold and beautiful.

And scary as hell.

Spending more time with Sam was what she wanted. Even though trying to work together was probably the worst thing for two people so drawn to each other because the temptation would still be there.

But she couldn't bring herself to end their partnership.

Couldn't tell him she didn't want to be with him when she did.

So, standing there in the crisp fall afternoon, she made herself a silent promise to keep a lid on her needs and wants. To deal with them after they closed the Windsor case. She was human, after all. That was the best she could do.

Looking back, she met Sam's waiting gaze. "We have dinner together, but we keep things focused on business. That goes for whenever we're together. Agreed?"

"Agreed," he said softly.

Spending Saturday evening in a candlelit Italian restaurant with Liz hadn't done anything to calm the need tethered tight inside Sam. Nor had the hours they'd spent hashing over the Windsor case brought any new leads to the forefront.

But the compromise he'd gotten Liz to agree to had given him what he wanted: more time with the compelling woman who had managed to tangle up his mind, crack the wall he'd built around his heart and made it seem worthwhile to take chances he'd vowed to never again take.

"Let's hope we strike pay dirt here."

Liz's comment snapped Sam's thoughts back to the present as she braked the detective cruiser beside a dusty pickup in the parking lot of P. R. Usher & Son Construction Company. It was Monday morning, and Brad Usher had responded to the message Liz left him on Friday. Usher had verified the company had been hired to do a job thirty years ago at David York's house. If they could wait a couple of hours, Usher would have his secretary dig the file out of the archives.

"We'd better strike something," Sam said while climbing out of the cruiser. "If we don't get names of the workers who had access to York's house, we're going to have a hell of a time finding out who wound up with the Colt."

If we ever find out, Liz thought darkly. Reviewing the Windsor investigation with Sam had convinced her this was the last viable lead they had to follow.

The outer office in the one-story building they entered was small and comfortably untidy. Manning a metal desk was a woman who wore a pair of pencils in her graying hair and an Usher & Son T-shirt. Liz instantly warmed to the woman's slightly harassed smile.

"Are you the police officers who phoned the boss?" she asked after putting her current caller on hold.

Liz nodded. "Sergeant Scott and Detective Broussard."

"Brad told me to send you back the instant you got here." The woman canted her chin toward a short hallway as two additional phone lines buzzed in unison. "It's Monday," she murmured before swiping up the receiver.

The man sitting behind the paper-strewn desk was toughly built with dark brown hair and looked to be in his early fifties. As he shook their hands, Liz decided Brad Usher had to be the son in the organization.

"My dad oversaw the job at David York's house," Usher said, confirming her theory while she and Sam settled in the two visitor chairs.

"Would he be available to talk to us?" Liz asked.

"I only wish. He died fifteen years ago." Usher opened a yellowed folder. "Dad always took pictures of the places where the company worked, just to help jog his memory about each site." Usher's mouth curved. "I didn't remember I'd worked on this job until I opened the file and saw the photo of the fountain with the naked mermaid."

Liz nodded. The burglar, J. D. Temple, had also remembered the fountain in the center of York's curved driveway. "This job was thirty years ago. You're sure you worked there?"

"Positive. I helped my dad during the summers when school was out. That gave me an early start in the business."

Liz opened the small notepad she'd pulled out of her tote bag. "Exactly what work did your company do at the York residence?"

"The customer had a detached garage with two parking bays. He hired us to add a third one."

"What else?" Liz prodded while jotting notes.

"Nothing else."

She looked up from her pad. "What about the renovation you did to the kitchen? And other areas inside the house?"

"Wasn't any."

"You're sure?"

While Usher shuffled through papers, Liz exchanged a quick look with Sam. His grim expression told her they were thinking the same thing. Judge York had claimed the construction crew had worked inside his house, which gave them access to his study and the desk from which the Colt had been stolen.

"Positive." Usher tapped the edges of the papers he'd gone through back into alignment. "We just worked on the garage."

The implications of what that meant to the Windsor investigation raced through Liz's head, but for the moment she pushed them away.

"Mr. Usher, not to malign your company's record-keeping, but is it possible that initially the job at the York residence involved only the addition to the garage? Then later the client asked your father to also do some renovation inside the main house?"

"If it was anyone but my dad, I'd say maybe. But he was a stickler for paperwork. I remember him sitting at our kitchen table almost every night, updating files on current jobs. If the work at the York home had involved renovating areas inside the main house, Dad would have made notes for the file."

"All right." Even though they weren't touching, Liz sensed that Sam's spine had gone as tense as hers. "Is there anything out of the ordinary about the job you remember? Anything unusual?"

"Not really." Usher closed the top flap on the folder. "Just that no one from Usher & Son had reason to set foot inside the main house."

"Well, well," Liz said as she slid into the cruiser's driver's seat. "It's not every day you catch a federal judge in a lie."

"First time for me," Sam said.

Drumming her fingers against the steering wheel, she stared out the windshield. She could feel adrenaline pumping into her bloodstream.

"We're both convinced that J. D. Temple didn't take

the Colt when he burglarized York's house," she said. "Now we can eliminate anyone from Usher stealing the gun. It's looking more and more like York still had the Colt in his possession on the date Geneviève Windsor was murdered."

"Looks like."

Liz was vaguely aware of the gruffness that had settled in Sam's voice, but her mind was working too fast for the implication to register.

"Thirty years ago, no one looked at York as a suspect," she continued. "There was no reason to since there was no known link between him and the victim. Still isn't. Now we start digging for one."

With sunlight streaming into the cruiser, she dug through her tote for her dark glasses. When she couldn't locate the case, she decided she must have left them on her desk. "York told us he hadn't owned the Colt long enough to fire it. If it's his skin and blood inside the gun, we'd have solid proof to contradict his claim."

"That still won't prove he shot Windsor."

"True, but if we can present undeniable evidence that he fired the murder weapon at some point, it will at least establish he lied to us. Why do that if he has nothing to hide?" She locked her seat belt into place. "We've got the DNA profile of the trace evidence found inside the gun. We need a sample of York's DNA for comparison."

"If we ask him for one, he'll close down like a trunk lid."

"Then we don't ask. With STR testing, the lab only

needs a minute amount to compile a DNA profile. It's legal for cops to obtain a known sample off of something discarded in public where there's no expectation of privacy. Like in a restaurant when a potential suspect throws away a used napkin or toothpick. Or at a reception held in a public venue, like the one tonight."

Liz pursed her mouth as she slid the key into the ignition and fired up the engine. "I'll make sure I get close enough to York to get something with his DNA on it."

"I told you, I don't like the idea of your being anywhere near the guy," Sam snapped in a voice so incredibly sharp it had edges.

Dropping her hand from the gearshift, she looked at him for the first time since they'd climbed back into the cruiser. His hands were fisted on his thighs, his mouth set in a grim line. His ghost-gray eyes looked as dark and hard as slate. She watched a muscle bunch underneath the tan skin of his jaw.

Liz felt her defenses go up like a drawbridge. The cop in her strained to point out that she currently had a .357 automatic holstered at her waist. That she'd been schooled in the same self-defense techniques as he, and she could damn well take care of herself. But she held herself back. Because Sam wasn't just her partner—he was the man she loved. And she discovered it didn't feel so bad to know he wanted to protect and defend her.

She remained silent, torn, tempted to reach over and take his hand. Work, she reminded herself after a moment. No personal business allowed.

She tilted her head. "So, I guess your cop vibes are still sending the message you need to protect me from the judge."

"You guess right," Sam grated.

He flexed his fingers, unflexed them. He didn't have to understand the prowling tension that left claw marks on his insides to heed it. Somehow, someway, York posed a threat to Liz. Period.

"We've already agreed there's something off about him," she said. "Maybe that's because both of us somehow knew York was going to turn into a suspect."

"Considering I have to fight the urge to draw my weapon anytime I'm around him, I'd say it's likely."

He raised a hand, dropped it back against his thigh. "This all might sound crazy, but I don't care."

"Sometimes it's hard to define what's crazy and what isn't," Liz said quietly. "I know how it is when something happens and there's no logical explanation or facts to explain it. Still, on some level you know it's real. So real, you're forced to deal with it."

Sam narrowed his eyes at the way her tone had softened. "Are you talking about something specific?"

"A dream." She massaged her left temple as if an ache had settled there. "Just this recurring dream I've had lately."

Which explained the shadows he'd seen so often under her eyes. "Want to tell me about it?"

"No." She lowered her hand, the corners of her mouth curving. "Because if I did, you'd think I had a screw or two loose. So I guess that makes us even."

"I'll have to take your word for it." Sam eased out a breath. "Look, I'm not trying to throw up a roadblock in our investigation. I know when a fire starts burning hot you have to feed it with any fuel available. In the Windsor case, that fuel is York's DNA."

"We have to have it, Sam. If I can get my captain's okay for us to get the sample, tonight's reception might be our only chance in the foreseeable future to legally obtain York's DNA."

"I know."

The car's interior had warmed and now Liz's feminine scent wrapped subtly about him, drawing him closer. It was a clean, soapy aroma that mingled with the warm sweetness of woman. Sam wanted to lean in and nuzzle her neck, to follow that faint scent to its source, investigate all the intriguing places where it might linger.

With his insides wound as tight as an addict's in withdrawal Sam told himself he'd been an absolute idiot to agree to keep things between them platonic. But he *had* agreed, dammit.

"If we get the go-ahead, I want you to make sure you stay in my sight while you talk to York," he said. "Don't try to pick up a toothpick or straw or anything else he's used. If he spots you doing that, he'll get suspicious. I'll deal with getting his DNA. You keep him distracted."

"That's a plan I can live with." Liz put the cruiser in gear and steered out of the parking lot. "Maybe our getting York's DNA will shove this case off high-center. I'm ready to get it solved."

Sam set his jaw while Liz drove through the late-morning traffic. Instinct told him it wasn't just his working partnership with her that faced an ending.

It was whatever they had in the past. Everything they might share in the future. *York can take it all away.*

The threat seemed so imminent, *so real,* Sam fisted his hands to keep from reaching for Liz.

Chapter 10

The reception sponsored by the Committee of One Hundred was held at Oklahoma City's most luxurious hotel.

Music swept around Sam and Liz the instant they entered the ornate lobby. Near the ballroom, a trio of harpists played interwoven melodies, accompanied by a pianist.

"No surprise in the choice of music," Liz said. While waiting for the sea of guests at the ballroom's arched entrance to thin out, she was aware of the firm press of Sam's palm at the small of her back.

And the subtle woodsy scent of his cologne.

Her pulse picking up speed, she slid him a look from beneath her lashes. Because he'd been on his way to a Colorado vacation, he didn't have a suit with him, just the gray sport coat and black slacks he'd paired with a starched white dress shirt. No tie. His dark hair was brushed back, the ends shaggy, his jaw freshly shaved. To Liz, he looked bad-guy handsome.

Judging from the speculative glances aimed his way from other female guests, she wasn't the only woman drawn to a man who looked lean, fit and dangerous.

"Why aren't you surprised by the music?" he asked.

Adjusting the strap on the clutch that held a small automatic and her badge, she shifted her thoughts. "According to Allie, a boatload of civic leaders belong to the committee. As do the executive director of the ballet company and the symphony, museum officials, oil company bigwigs, doctors, lawyers and judges. Not the type of membership to go for your standard-issue bump-and-grind tunes."

"True." Sam's eyes scanned the crowd as cop's eyes do—measuring, detailing, filing. "Give me a cold beer and Cajun music, and I'm in heaven."

With cypress trees and Spanish moss thick in his voice, Liz easily pictured him kicked back in some dimly lit Louisiana watering hole. Which was where he'd probably head as soon as they closed the Windsor investigation.

The sudden thought of their being separated by so many miles had her insides knotting. Her breathing shallowed. Not even at the end of her relationship with Andrew had she felt this twisting, this aching, the shaky fear of losing.

Sam's head angled while his gray eyes narrowed on her face. "You okay?"

"Fine." She had to take a breath so her voice would stay steady. She wouldn't think about how things would be after they cleared the case. *Couldn't* bear to think about them.

"Any sign of the judge?" she asked when they moved deeper into the ballroom where crystal chandeliers spilled light over the crowd. A circle of linen-covered tables loaded with hors d'oeuvres sat in the center of the room. Inside the circle was another table holding an enormous 100 carved in ice that shimmered like diamonds.

Liz noted that most of the men wore dark suits, the women were in cocktail dresses or suits. She sent up silent thanks to Allie for lending her the short jacket in rich emerald silk and elegant black tuxedo pants that made Liz feel like she fit in with the highbrow crowd.

"He's at the right of the buffet table," Sam said quietly.

Shifting sideways, Liz peered through the crowd. She spotted their quarry sipping champagne while conversing with a matronly-looking woman with brown hair scraped back into a tight bun. York's black suit looked as if it had been tailored to his lanky frame; his silver hair gleamed beneath the lights. Liz knew that the majority of people watching him would see a distinguished-looking, renowned jurist who exuded power.

She saw a possible killer.

"I don't think I can sneak his honor's champagne glass out of here under my jacket," Sam said, his voice low to keep from being overheard. "We'll have to get his DNA off of something else."

"I'll hit the buffet table, then get his attention. After that, I'll play it by ear."

"*We'll* play it by ear," Sam corrected. "His honor isn't going to be happy to see me, so I'll stay out of his range of sight. If it looks like there's going to be a problem getting the sample, I'll move in."

"All right."

When Liz started to step away, Sam's hand settled at her waist. "Be careful." His eyes stayed locked on hers as he eased closer. "Whether or not you buy into the hinky feeling I have about York doesn't matter. We're here because he may have murdered a woman. That's reason enough for us to keep our guard up."

Through her jacket, she felt the pressure of Sam's fingers against her waist. For a fleeting instant she wondered what they would feel like against her bare flesh.

"I don't plan to take any unnecessary chances," she said softly.

While she excused her way toward the center of the ballroom, Liz recognized some faces from the newspaper's society pages, but didn't run into anyone she knew. On the other hand, Allie, with her unlimited wealth and social connections, would probably be acquainted with everyone in attendance.

Liz reached the opposite side of the buffet table

from York. She picked up a small plate and began to fill it, purposely bypassing the finger-size quiches. Instead she used party toothpicks with plastic swirls on one end to spear cubes of cheese, shrimp and a pastry-wrapped hors d'oeuvre she couldn't identify.

Slowly she made her way around the ring of tables. She met York's gaze just as the matronly woman excused herself and moved off.

"Judge York."

"Sergeant Scott." He approached her, his smile all charm. "How delightful to see you. I would have been disappointed if you hadn't come tonight."

"I looked forward to this," she said with complete honesty. If he'd killed Windsor, getting his DNA might be the first step in proving that. Using a pick, she speared a piece of cheese off her plate, slid it into her mouth.

He motioned with his own champagne glass. "Can I get you a drink?"

Her gaze flicked past York's shoulder. Sam stood a few feet behind the judge, speaking quietly to a waiter. The man nodded, then moved off.

Liz shook her head. "Thanks, I've already got a drink on the way."

"Very well." Smoothly York sipped his champagne. "Earlier, I discussed your work with several committee members who supported me in obtaining the grant that funds the cold case office."

She popped a shrimp into her mouth. "Is that so?"

"I told them you interviewed me about my stolen

Colt because it was the same caliber as the weapon used in an unsolved murder from thirty years ago. My associates were intrigued as to the status of your investigation. I told them I would inquire."

"The investigation is ongoing."

He inclined his head. "As a judge, I understand you can't divulge sensitive information. Suffice it to say that I hope my inability to locate the name of the construction company that worked inside my home hasn't hampered your ability to solve the murder. It would be a huge coup for the committee to know its efforts are showing positive results after so short a time."

"When it comes to murder, I don't let much slow me down, Judge."

"David, please, in such a friendly setting," he said, touching her elbow. A chill, very brief but very real, shot up Liz's spine. "Then you might permit me to call you Elizabeth."

The way he said her name just added to the creep factor. With York's dark eyes locked on hers, she didn't dare glance again at Sam. "Liz." She forced a smile. "Call me Elizabeth again, I might have to shoot you."

York chuckled. "Liz, it is."

The way his gaze crawled over her increased her gnawing sense of urgency to get York's DNA then put distance between them. She'd felt uneasy around suspects before, but the vague, undefined anxiety that now darkened the back reaches of her mind had her stomach in knots. Did that feeling seem so much more intense because she believed there was something to Sam's instinctive suspicion of York?

Liz sampled one of the pastry-wrapped hors d'oeuvres she'd put on her plate.

"I don't know what this is," she said, giving York a quizzical look. She gestured toward the buffet table where a tray of the same hors d'oeuvres sat. "David, would you mind tasting one of those and telling me what's in them?"

"I'd be happy to."

When York stepped to the table, Liz glanced to where Sam had been standing. He was no longer in sight. Still, she sensed his presence, felt his gaze on her, as sure as a touch.

York returned, holding a small plate with two of the hors d'oeuvres. He tasted one, laid the pick onto his plate. "Paté wrapped in pastry with a touch of fresh thyme, I believe."

"Okay." The knots in Liz's stomach tightened. She had to fight the urge to grab the pick off his plate and bolt for the nearest door. "I just survived my first encounter with paté and lived to tell about it."

"So it seems." York took another sip of champagne, then raised a salt and pepper brow. "Did you say you had a drink coming?"

"It's here." Sam stepped up, purposely positioning himself close to Liz as he handed her a glass of tonic water.

For Sam, it seemed that his and Liz's thoughts had been linked the entire time she'd been in York's presence. Somehow, someway, Sam had felt her discomfort grow with every passing second. And when York tasted the bite-size appetizer and dropped the pick on the plate he still held, Sam could have sworn he and Liz experienced the same lightning bolt of adrenaline.

Now, all they needed was to get the pick coated with York's DNA off the bastard's plate.

"Detective Broussard," York said. "I had no idea you'd be here tonight."

Sam had seen more pleasant smiles on the faces of felons he'd busted. "I hope my presence is a nice surprise." The look he and York exchanged was utterly adversarial, their eyes locked, dark brown to gray flint.

"But of course." York drank, then inclined his head. "When you and Liz came to my chambers, you mentioned you were trying to ascertain if the man who burglarized my home three decades ago had also committed crimes in Shreveport. I assumed you would have found that answer by now and returned there."

York's use of Liz's first name made Sam want to bare his teeth and show some fang. Easing closer to her, he gripped her elbow in the same spot he'd seen York place his hand. *Want to erase the bastard's touch.* "I plan to stay in Oklahoma City until Liz and I get all of our business taken care of."

York's mouth pressed into a thin line. "Well, Detective, since we have such a compelling woman in common, I expect we'll meet again."

"Count on it, Judge."

York turned to Liz. "I hope to see you again soon."

He looked deeply into her eyes, held the moment. "Very soon."

"Something tells me you will," she said.

York walked away. Sam tracked his movements, and felt his spine stiffen when the judge sat his champagne glass and plate with a few others on a tray table.

"That was all around creepy." Liz gestured toward the table with her drink. "Let's get the pick."

"After you."

At the tray, Liz set her plate and glass aside while Sam reached into the pocket of his sport coat and pulled out one of the small envelopes he'd picked up from the forensic lab. While Liz blocked the view of inquiring eyes, he sealed the pick inside the envelope, then slipped it into his pocket.

And then he turned. She stood waiting for him, her green eyes luminous beneath the bright lights, her lustrous, copper-colored hair restrained in an intricate braid. He took in her emerald-colored jacket, made of some rich fabric that clung to every curve, the whispering black silk of the tuxedo pants.

For so long he'd been slogging through each day, trying to get things right. But it hit him now that he didn't feel like he was slogging when he was with Liz. He felt alive.

He hadn't fought for Tanya, he knew that. He wished things between them had been different, but truth be told, after their marriage started falling apart he just hadn't cared enough.

Liz was different. Just the idea of losing her ripped a hole in his heart.

"Ready to head to the lab?" she asked.

The sense of danger around her was like a bony finger skimming up Sam's spine. He struggled against the feral instinct that told him to pull her to him. Hold her. *Protect.*

He settled for pressing his palm against the small of her back. "Yeah," he said quietly. "Let's get the hell out of here."

The dream returned in the dark hours before dawn, enshrouding Liz in a sensuous haze.

Dream Lover leaned over her, his eyes like aquamarines, as vivid as the sea. She struggled to see more than just his eyes as his powerful body moved between her thighs, his hips hammering rhythmically at her, driving deep.

But the slivers of moonlight coming through the windows were so weak she was helpless to see him. She could only feel him possessing her so fiercely, so completely that she knew she would never be free of him.

Never wanted to be.

He pushed deeper and she moaned. His taste was hot, tart and uncivilized and now, shatteringly familiar. But not just as an echo from the past. The vision of a man's face formed in her mind, Sam's face. But his eyes were incendiary-blue, not flint-gray.

Reeling with shock, she struggled against Dream Lover's grasp.

"Sae wit be wel bewared! Touche not wat se cyning woulde enfeffe."

The warning in his voice was unmistakable, roughened by passion. Was it Sam's voice? She couldn't tell. All she could do was feel the tremors of emotion in the hands locked onto her waist.

Helplessly she clutched his shoulders as lightning bolts of pure, white heat shot through her. She wanted to curl her legs around his hips, but she could no longer move. Her world narrowed until she became pure sensation.

All at once the moonlight dimmed. The air against her damp flesh went cold: There, in the darkened corner of her bedroom, something moved stealthily.

Fear gushed like acid in her veins.

He was coming! Slinking like a shadow, an inky formless shape edging closer and closer. Soon his breath would be on the back of her neck; soon his hand would curl around her throat.

"Who are you?" She screamed the words out in a voice in her head.

And then she saw the pale glint of moonlight off the gun's barrel.

"No!"

Liz bolted upright out of sleep, her hand groping for the automatic on her nightstand. Lungs heaving, she fought the twisted sheet from around her legs and lunged off the bed.

Gun aimed toward the darkest corner of her bedroom, she used a trembling hand to fumble on the bedside lamp.

The bedroom that she'd softened with pillows and bright fabrics looked just as it should. The drawers on the washed pine dresser were tidily shut. She'd left the closet door ajar when she'd gone to bed and she could see the array of her clothing hung in a disciplined parade of colors.

Everything was as it should be, except her big iron bed. It looked like it had been ransacked, the sheet and blankets twisted around each other. Every one of her pillows had wound up on the floor.

"Hell." Still clutching her automatic, Liz lowered her arm. She dragged in a deep breath, trying to get her balance back.

Tonight's dream had been more intense than all the others. In truth, it hadn't felt anything like a dream. Dream Lover's voice had sounded so real. *He'd* been real. His taste…

Her eyes widened as details came flooding back. His taste had been Sam's. The face that had formed in her mind had been Sam's, his flinty-gray eyes having somehow transformed to blue.

Had it all been wishful thinking on her part? Brought about by her maddening erotic imaginings of what it would be like to make love with her temporary partner?

Surely that was it, because, holy heaven, she'd never had such intense sex in her life as she'd had tonight with a total figment of her imagination. It was as though Dream Lover had sucked every ounce of resistance out of her and replaced it with live, crackling electricity and primal satisfaction.

She eased onto the edge of the mattress and stared at the room's far corner, now illuminated with soft light. She had sensed someone there. Someone evil. *Coming for her.*

Liz couldn't stop the chill from streaking up her spine. She was alone, she assured herself. Her loft apartment, along with the rest of The Montgomery, was safe and sound and cloaked in silence.

Setting her automatic aside, she used both hands to shove her long hair away from her face. She was exhausted, totally spent. And although her mind and body ached with fatigue, she knew from experience she wouldn't be able to shake off the sticky dregs of the dream and fall back to sleep.

Dropping her face into her hands, she tried to steady her breathing while she wondered what the hell she was going to do. Was she slowly going crazy? Flailing around in some psychotic pit she'd stumbled into?

She dragged in a breath, struggling against a spurt of panic. The dream wasn't going to stop on its own, she was convinced of that now. Tomorrow, she would make an appointment with the department's shrink. She had no choice.

From outside, she heard the clock in the tower in the center of Reunion Square bong the half hour. And while she sat alone on her big iron bed, Dream Lover's voice crept into her mind.

"Sae wit be wel bewared! Touche not wat se cyning woulde enfeffe."

Liz's spine went as straight as string. She remembered! *Finally* she remembered what Dream Lover kept saying!

Heart hammering, she jerked open the drawer on her nightstand. Then muttered a curse when she remembered she'd used the last page of the notepad she habitually kept there.

She rushed out of her bedroom and headed downstairs, taking the steps two at a time. The wooden floor cool against her bare feet, she flicked on the kitchen light, jerked open a drawer and grabbed paper and pen.

She dashed off the foreign-sounding words with a shaking hand, not bothering to try to figure out how to spell them. She had struggled for so long to remember everything Dream Lover said, she would settle for having the words down in any form.

Later, she would figure out what to do with them.

A sharp knock on the front door nearly sent her jumping out of her skin. Who the hell would be knocking on her door at almost three o'clock in the morning?

On the heels of that thought, came the possibility that something had happened to either Allie or Claire.

Still, the cop in Liz took time to jerk out another drawer in the kitchen and grab the small automatic she'd carried in her purse to the reception. Another sharp rap sounded. As she padded to the door, she jacked a round into the automatic's chamber, a sharp, ratcheting noise in the high-ceiling loft.

Easing sideways, she peered through the peephole. And felt her heart clench when she saw Sam standing in the hallway.

His appearance in tonight's dream had disconcerted her. She didn't want to see him now, not when she felt so vulnerable, exposed, confused.

But he wouldn't have shown up at such an ungodly hour for no reason.

She unlocked the dead bolt, swung open the door. He wore gray drawstring pants, a sweatshirt with Shreveport P.D. emblazoned across the front and running shoes. No socks. His gray eyes looked as hard as granite, a rough shadow of beard darkened his cheeks and jaw, his hair was disheveled, his mouth grim.

"What are you doing here?" She whispered the words in deference to her neighbors.

"We need to talk."

He strode in, then just stood there, saying nothing, his gaze focused on her like a laser.

Feeling like a bug under a microscope, she was suddenly aware she'd bypassed putting on her robe before rushing downstairs. Standing there in the boxers and thin tank top she habitually slept in, Liz felt defenseless.

"Talk…about what?"

His gaze flicked to her right hand. "How about putting that automatic away first?"

And because she hated feeling at a loss of control, she raised her chin. "I wouldn't have answered the door armed if you'd have called to tell me you were coming."

Turning, she walked to the sitting area and laid the

gun on one of the tables beside the couch. It hit her that she still had the paper with Dream Lover's words clenched in her hand.

When she turned, Sam was standing only a few feet away. He'd moved so stealthily, she hadn't heard his steps.

"You're right, I should have called." He jabbed a hand through his dark hair, leaving it even more tousled. "I didn't think about it because when I jerked awake from the dream I had, all I knew was I had to see you. Talk to you in person."

Liz hesitated. "You had a dream?"

"That's how it started out." He shook his head. "It changed, became more than just a dream. It was real. At least to me it was."

He stepped closer, his gaze steady on hers. "This is going to sound crazy. Crazier than anything I've told you before, but I swear it's the truth. We were together tonight, Liz. We made love."

"That's not possible." Whatever it was in her subconscious that created Dream Lover had done so weeks before she knew that Sam Broussard existed. Not until she'd met him, kissed him, had she started imagining the similarities between him and Dream Lover.

"I don't care if it's possible or not," Sam said. The frustration in his voice shone in his face. "All I know is I was here with you." His gaze lifted. "Upstairs in your bed. *Your big iron bed.* I felt you, Liz. I was inside you. I heard you moan."

"I…" He had only been to her loft one other time,

but he hadn't ventured upstairs to her bedroom. *How could he know she had an iron bedstead?*

"Listen to me." He gripped her shoulders, his fingers hard and firm. "In the dream, or whatever the hell it was, I remember what I said to you. It was in some language I can't speak, and I have no idea what the words mean. I just know I said them."

Liz's legs began to tremble. Control, she ordered herself, but knew the only reason she was still standing was Sam's firm grip on her shoulders.

"In the dream, what did you say?" Her voice was thick, unsteady.

"Sae wit be wel bewared. Touche not wat se cyning woulde enfeffe."

"Oh, God." She jerked from his grip, took a step back. "How could you know that?"

"Beats me." His forehead furrowed. "You've heard that before? In the same language?"

She nodded. And because words failed her, she offered him the paper. Wrapping her arms around her waist, she watched his face as he scanned the words. Saw his eyes narrow.

"Did you hear those words in a dream, too?" he asked, looking up from the paper.

"A lot of dreams. I could never recall more than a couple of words. Tonight I remembered everything, so I wrote it down."

"Is this the recurring dream you've mentioned? The one that's caused you to lose sleep? Were we together in those dreams, too?"

"No. I never thought the man in my dreams was you until…"

"Until?"

"The other night when we kissed. That's when I started wondering." She shoved her heavy mass of hair behind her shoulders. "His eyes are the same shape as yours, but they're brilliant blue, not gray. How could he be you when the dream started before we ever met?"

"I don't know."

"Wait a minute," she said as realization blew through her in a sudden spurt. "Could your grandmother have done this?"

His brows snapped up. "My grandmother?"

"I have no clue what a conjure woman is capable of, but maybe she decided to do some—" Liz flicked her wrist, groping for words "—psychic matchmatching to get you back into the dating pool."

"My grandmother senses things about people. She mixes herbs and reads tarot cards. She can't open a mental door into a person's mind and will them to think certain thoughts. Or dream specific dreams." Sam scrubbed a hand over the back of his neck. "Which right now makes me very glad, because I don't even want to consider the possibility my grandmother had anything to do with the hottest dream I've had since puberty hit."

"Okay." Giving in to fatigue and nerves, Liz dropped onto the couch. "I'm just trying to make some sense of all this."

"Maybe we can do that together."

Massaging the birthmark on the inside of her wrist, she looked up at him. "How?"

"We're cops." Sam settled on the couch beside her. "We approach this like any investigation—ask questions, dig for answers." In the wash of light coming from the kitchen, his face looked tense, his eyes serious. "Tell me about your dream, Liz. When did it begin?"

"The night Andrew and I went to Vegas and I discovered I couldn't get down the aisle of the chapel. We called off our engagement and I flew back here."

Weary, she rested her head against the back of the couch. "I jolted awake at two o'clock. Even though I knew I was dreaming, physically, everything felt so real that I thought some guy had broken in and climbed into bed with me. And he spoke to me, but I couldn't understand what he said. But I didn't care. All I cared about was what he was doing to me. How he made me feel."

She saw a muscle tighten in Sam's jaw, but he remained silent.

"About a week ago, the dream changed. He had a gun."

"What kind?"

"I don't know. It has a stainless steel finish because the moonlight glints off the barrel." She frowned. "He doesn't point it at me. He just raises his hand and the gun's there."

She dragged her fingers through her hair. "Always at the end of the dream, the air goes cold. And there's someone else there with me." She felt the power of his evilness as she spoke. "Someone dark and malignant, lurking in the shadows."

"Have you seen him?" Sam asked quietly.

"No, I always bolt awake right then."

"The first man in your dreams, what does he look like?"

"I don't know. All I've ever been able to make out are his eyes." She slid Sam a sideways look. "At least until tonight."

"You saw his face?"

"I saw *your* face, Sam. But your eyes were blue like his, not gray. And when he kissed me, I tasted you. But that isn't possible because you weren't here."

"Not physically," he agreed. "Mentally's a different matter."

Liz was tempted to argue the point, but she couldn't. Otherwise, how would Sam remember saying the exact words she'd written down in a language neither of them spoke?

"If that's the case," Sam continued, "am I the guy who's shown up in your dreams every night?"

"How could you be?" she asked, twisting on the couch to face him. "How could I have dreamed about you before I ever knew you existed?"

He reached out, took her hand in his. "The same way I dreamed about you years ago."

"You what?"

"When I was a kid, I had this recurring dream of a young girl with red hair. We were friends, played innocent childhood games. My grandmother insisted my subconscious playmate was 'in my blood,' as she put it. After each dream, Grandmother mixed up an herb bag and placed it under my pillow."

Liz furrowed her brow. "What were the herbs supposed to do?"

"Ward off bad spirits." The soft graze of his thumb over her knuckles sent a surge of warmth up Liz's spine. "As I got older, so did the girl in my dreams. Then I turned into a randy teenager with far different needs. My feelings for the redheaded girl were no longer platonic, and I didn't know how to deal with all that, so I managed to block the dreams. Finally they stopped, and I forgot about them. And her."

His touch was doing crazy things to her pulse rate, but the last thing Liz wanted to do was pull away. She needed the soothing warmth of his touch.

"When did you remember the dreams?" she prodded. "And the redheaded girl?"

"The day I showed up here with the Colt and watched you rush toward me in the P.D.'s basement. I knew without a doubt that the girl in my dreams was you."

"How can that be?"

"It just is."

When she started to protest, he lifted her hand, pressed a soft kiss to her knuckles. "My grandmother would say this is the point where we have to stop thinking like cops because logic and facts don't apply," he murmured. "We just have to accept."

Accept this, Liz thought, or accept insanity.

"I can tell you one thing with certainty," Sam said, his breath a warm wash against her knuckles.

"What?" she asked, struggling to absorb the impossible into reality. "What can you tell me, Sam?"

"I've wanted you for what feels like an eternity."

The raw emotion in his eyes had her yielding like wax. With desire flowing through every cell of her body, she lifted her free hand and cupped her palm against the side of his throat. Was he Dream Lover? That she was even asking herself that question seemed surreal.

What she knew for sure was that Sam Broussard was real—all muscle and sinew and musky smelling male. She had never felt so in tune, so close to any man, as with him.

He turned her hand over to press a slow, warm kiss to her palm, and her breath caught. This was right, she thought, nearly groaning in erotic pleasure. Their being together was right.

She rose off the couch. "Let's go upstairs," she said softly, tightening her fingers on his. "I want you to see my big iron bed in person."

Chapter 11

Sam had thought he understood desire well. But when he stepped into Liz's dimly lit bedroom where her scent hung on the air, he couldn't remember ever having it ram into him with such force that it took his breath away.

She paused beside him, their fingers linked. When she gazed up at him, her green eyes glistened in the pale light. He could swear he felt electricity coursing from her hand straight to his gut.

"Is that the same bed as the one in your dream, Sam?"

He glanced across the room to the iron bed with slim, smooth posts that framed both the head and foot of the mattress. The blankets and sheet were twisted together, the pillows strewn on the wood floor, testimony to Liz's own tumultuous dream.

"That's it." He reached out, just a whisper of fingers on her face. "This time, it's only you and me," he said in a low voice. "There's no one else here. No one conjured up from either of our subconscious."

His soft touch was somehow wildly passionate, desperately intimate. Liz shivered from a frisson of excitement, anticipation, the sexual buzz that heated her blood whenever he was near.

She cupped her palm to his cheek. "Only us," she murmured.

Swept up by need, they came together as suddenly as a spark to dry kindling, igniting like a flash of flame. Then they burned, wild and frenzied, their movements driven by wants and desires they'd both held at bay.

His impatient hands peeled off her thin tank top. Hers shoved up his sweatshirt and T-shirt in one tangle, yanking them over his head.

The dim light shone against the bronze planes of his chest. Her hands and fingers were pale against his skin, the contrast wildly arousing, as was the knowledge his heartbeat was as erratic as her own. Lowering her head, she pressed her mouth against his shoulder. The familiar taste of him filled her senses as she traced her tongue across his collarbone, down through the dark swirls of hair.

Sam's hand dived into her long tresses, fisted there. He'd been certain he couldn't want her more than he had earlier at the reception when he realized what it would mean to lose her. But this was different. She was *everything,* he realized as a raw, aching need filled him, throbbing in his loins. With the fiery strands clinging to his hand and wrist like licks of flame, he watched her tongue stroking his chest. And hissed out a breath when he felt the wet velvet of her lips at his nipple. No part of his system was spared the rapid on-slaught of that lush and knowing mouth.

Liz felt his muscles bunch, heard him groan her name. Then his hands locked on her waist, nudging her back. His warm fingers circled her breasts, his lips closed over a taut nipple. The heat of his mouth was wild, burning with wet fire as he drew the erect bud between his teeth and gently nibbled. Trembling, she plunged her fingers through his dark hair, pulling him to her other breast.

Her flesh ached and hummed with an urgency that spread downward from the gentle tugging at her breast to the awakening pulse at her womb. When his mouth left her, she gasped with the sudden ache of loss, only to draw her breath in sharply at the sensation of his lips just above the waist of her boxers.

She felt the insistent tug of his fingers as he peeled the shorts off her hips. While his hands stroked her bare flesh, his mouth took hers.

There was no tenderness in him now. He was all hunger, barely controlled, his skin hot against hers, his mouth demanding.

She opened for him, wanting to taste that heat, to

taste all of him. She moaned as need became a heavy throb deep inside her. Then his mouth moved over her flesh in an urgent whispered need of his own.

He savored the taste of the skin at her neck, cool and shadowed beneath her hair where it lay at her shoulders. He pushed the coppery mass back with one hand as his other pulled her closer. He indulged himself in her scent while running his tongue down the curve of her throat to the slope of her shoulder. Gently he closed his teeth over the silken ridge of flesh.

Liz shuddered against the jagged, savage thrill that ripped through her. Desperate to have him, she tugged at the drawstring of his sweatpants while he fought off his shoes. Her fingers tangled with his as he stripped off the sweatpants and she discovered that he wore nothing underneath. He was dark and bronze all over, including the thick, erect flesh that stood up against his hard, flat belly.

She felt the iron-hard tension in his arms as he lifted her.

For a moment, the shapes and colors in the room seemed to shift out of sync. And in that surrealistic instant, Sam gazed down at her with eyes that looked incendiary-blue. *Dream Lover blue.*

Somewhere in the vague recesses of her mind she knew she should try to logic out the meaning of that. But not now when his mouth was on hers, taking her away from reason, muddling her thoughts and driving a kaleidoscope of feelings to the surface where she couldn't escape them.

She was softness and light, Sam thought as he settled with her onto the disheveled bed. Her long hair spread like a red-gold river over the white sheet. He fanned his fingers low over her belly, grazed his thumb over the hardened nub of flesh between her soft folds. Like molten silver, she flowed under his touch. Gently he parted those layers; his other hand moved low at her back as he lifted her hips and entered her.

Darkness and light, night and day, fire and ice. For Sam, they came together in a wild torrent of desire.

Beneath him she was slender and strong, her curves and softness yielding, drawing him in, even as those clear green eyes drew in his soul. Words wouldn't come to him. He didn't think he could explain what he was feeling—that she touched something deep inside him, made him feel when no one had made him feel anything in a very long time. He wanted the kind of strength that seemed to come so naturally to her, yet at the same time he felt that searing, urgent need to protect her.

Need. All of his senses sharpened and focused on that single word. And now it seemed it had been inside him always, waiting. His need for this one woman.

A groan strangled in his throat when she arched her hips and took him deeper still. She's mine, he thought dimly while his body shuddered. This time, for all time, *mine.*

When he sensed the first faint spasms beginning deep inside her, he knew he could have easily followed her. Instead he gritted his teeth and held on to control.

Lacing his fingers through hers, he drew their clasped hands over her head, marveling at the strength in her slender hands as she panted his name.

Nuzzling her throat, he waited for her body to cool, for passion to subside in those cat-green eyes.

When she lay limp and spent, he began again. Her fingers flexed against his, locking around the rungs of the iron bed while her head whipped to the side. Fascinated, he watched the transformation from cool ice to molten fire, wanting only to fulfill her needs, and in doing so fulfill his own.

Her body moved with his, matching each smooth stroke. He quickened the rhythm, heard the husky moan slip up her throat as passion inside her built and vivid pleasure glazed her eyes.

"Let it happen," he said, his voice a husky rasp.

"Not…without you this time," she panted.

"Not without me."

He watched her eyes go dark, felt the powerful spasms that pulsed once more through her body.

Only then did he follow her.

She was hot and wet and constant fluid motion, rising to meet him like a siren out of the sea. Her long legs wrapped around him, her husky voice moaned his name, her green eyes filled with lust. He pushed deeper and she—

Sam jerked awake, instantly lifting his head from the mattress. The clock on the nightstand glowed a red six. He lowered his face back to the mattress with a groan. Between making love with Liz, then *dreaming* about it, he was surprised he could even move.

He was exhausted. Weak as a baby. And he was alone.

Which was the last thing he wanted to be.

Rolling onto his back, he puffed out a breath. Because he'd grown up in a family that believed in tarot readings, herb bags and trinkets, he now wholly accepted that some sort of telepathic connection existed between himself and Liz. He couldn't explain what it was, or how it had come about. Couldn't apply logic to it. It just was.

He knew one other thing that *just was*. He had fallen in love.

Which was something he had vowed he would never do again. Hell, after Tanya, he'd sworn off women altogether—that had been the only way he could deal with the guilt of having failed as a husband and protector. Now, here he was, in love with a woman who all of his instincts told him he needed to defend.

The new feelings swirling inside him were going to take some getting used to.

Sam eased out of bed. After hitting the rest room he pulled on his sweatpants and was about to head downstairs when Liz swept into the bedroom, bringing the rich aroma of coffee with her.

She wore a white terry robe that hung to her ankles. A clip anchored her thick hair up in a disheveled topknot. A laptop computer was tucked under one arm, and in each hand she carried a mug with steam rising off its top.

"You won't believe what I found." Her voice was all business, her eyes somber as she handed him a mug. In what Sam sensed was almost an afterthought, she rose on tiptoes and pecked him on the cheek.

He may need a little more time to get used to the new feelings that had rocked him, but that didn't mean he planned to maintain distance. So when she started to turn away, he captured her chin between his thumb and fingers, halting her steps. No matter what she had found, it couldn't be more monumental than what they had shared over the past hours.

"Good morning," he murmured.

"Hi, I'm sort of on an—" Her words died out when he lowered his mouth to hers.

He kept the kiss soft, smooth, seductive. Endlessly patient, he parted her lips with teasing nips and nibbles. Degree by torturous degree, he deepened the kiss until her free hand clutched at his waist and her body shuddered.

"You're on a what?" he asked softly.

"Investigative…roll," she breathed. Her face was flushed, her eyes smoky.

His thumb traced the curve of her lower lip. "Why don't you tell me about it?"

She took an unsteady step back. "It would be easier to do that if you hadn't just kissed me senseless."

"My pleasure." He flashed her a grin before taking a sip of coffee. "The investigator in me wanted to know if you're the type of woman who wants hearts and flowers after a night of making love."

Her gaze slid to the bed, her forehead furrowing. "I didn't think I was."

"Then I guess we both have a lot to learn about each other. And ourselves, too."

She shook her head as if to clear the fog. "You're right. Plus, we still have a murder to solve."

"Agreed." He nodded at the laptop still trapped under her arm. "What did you find that put you on an investigative roll?"

"Something you won't believe." Abandoning her mug to the nightstand, she climbed onto the bed and opened the laptop's lid.

Sam snagged pillows off the floor and propped them against the iron headboard before settling beside her.

"I wanted to know what language is spoken in both our dreams," she said while entering a few keystrokes. "So, I hit the Internet."

"Good idea."

"It's middle English, which equates to medieval English."

Sam's hand froze with his coffee mug halfway to his mouth. *"Medieval,"* he repeated. "Here we are, dealing with a homicide suspect who writes books on the law in medieval times."

"Spooky, isn't it?" Liz asked while entering data. "Don't forget about the bracelet with the fire opal that J. D. Temple stole from York's house."

Sam set his mug on the nightstand while pulling back the information Claire Castle found about the red gem that, in medieval times, was considered a symbol of the most fervent love between a man and a woman. He gazed at Liz's birthmark that matched Temple's sketch of the bracelet's wide gold band, twisted to form lovers' knots.

"I haven't forgotten," he said evenly.

Liz shoved at her loose topknot. "I don't remember all the details about the legend connected with the bracelet. Something about a love triangle involving a young woman, a knight and an older guy. Said older guy killed the other two and had a spell cast that would keep them apart throughout eternity."

"You hit the main points." Too many, Sam thought. There were too many things linking himself and Liz—and now York—for the connections to be shrugged off.

"There's one main point missing," Liz said. "That bracelet keeps coming up, but there's nothing to tie it to our investigation. York owned it, but for some reason he didn't report it stolen. Then some masked man robbed the fence who bought the bracelet from Temple. It's a dead end."

"So far," Sam agreed. "Any idea what the words in our dreams mean?"

"Not yet," Liz said, her gaze fixed on the computer's screen. "I'm making a run now using a different search engine."

After a pause she said, "Okay, here's the translation. 'This law is well-known. Touch not what the king would enfief.'"

"Not the usual conversation one shares during lovemaking."

"In my dream, he…*you*," Liz amended, sliding him a sideways look, "makes it sound urgent. It's some sort of warning."

When she glanced back at the laptop's screen, her eyes went wide. "Holy cow."

"What?"

"You know that Web site that has the *see inside the book* feature?"

"Yeah."

"I just got a hit, meaning the same medieval language from both our dreams is also in a book. Guess who wrote it?"

Considering the way Liz's voice had gone dead serious, Sam didn't need to guess. "York, our resident expert of medieval law."

"Right." Liz's eyes turned wary. "Sam, how can that be? How could you and I have separate dreams with the same foreign-sounding language in them? Language that's also in a book written by our prime suspect in the Windsor case?"

Before he could answer, she shook her head. "I can't believe I'm asking this, but do you think we're in some strange reincarnation situation?"

"Sounds that way." Sam eased out a breath. "We both have sensed we've met sometime in the past, but neither of us can peg where or when. Reincarnation would at least explain that."

"And make things even more weird," Liz added. Her eyes probed his face. "What do *you* think, Sam?"

"That we'll never know for sure, so we should concentrate on this lifetime because it's the only one we have control over." He paused for a moment. "Let's talk about what brought us together."

"The Windsor case."

He nodded. "It sat cold for thirty years until I recovered the murder weapon. The minute I touched the Colt, I felt an intense edginess for the first time in years."

"Okay, so the day you found the Colt, things started changing. You felt different."

"Right." Instinctively he picked up her thought processes. "When did things start changing for you?"

She tapped keys on the laptop, turned it toward him and pointed to a date on the calendar displayed on the screen. "The day I was supposed to marry Andrew the first time."

Sam felt his mouth go dry. "That's the same day I recovered the Colt."

Liz regarded him in dismay. "Are you thinking what I am? That we'd be fooling ourselves if we said those two events aren't somehow cosmically connected?"

"Sounds like it."

She pointed to another date on the screen. "This is the day you first called to tell me you'd recovered a weapon that ballistics linked to the Windsor case. That was the day Andrew and I flew to Vegas."

She shifted against the pillows to face him. Her skin was pale, her eyes strained. "I was ready to get married on both those dates. I didn't have any doubts. But I couldn't make it down the aisle either time. Then the dream started. I didn't know what to think then. I don't know what to think now."

"I think," Sam began quietly, "we can't depend on logic and facts for this. Only feelings and instinct, which tell me that fate meant us to be here." He reached up, slid the clip from her hair and watched the red waterfall tumble over her shoulders. "Together like this."

"Fate sounds like a better explanation for what's happened than a stress-induced break with reality." Liz rested a hand against his bare chest. "Sam, you know how in every investigation there are certain things that never get explained? Holes that never get filled in? Despite them, you still make your case. Arrest the bad guy."

"Yeah, I know."

"I vote that's how we deal with all of this unexplainable stuff for now. It's all freaky but it doesn't change the fact we have a murder to solve. So, we keep the investigation on track. Hope that the checks we've started running on York uncover a connection between him and Geneviève Windsor."

"And the unexplainable stuff?"

"Like you said, we have no control over it. So, we set it aside mentally. Deal with it only if we have to."

"Works for me," Sam said, even as his jaw clenched. He was certain something evil lurked just out of his vision. Something dark, growing with the cancerous speed of a brewing storm, waiting to ooze out of its shadowy hiding place.

That certainty sent a preternatural chill stirring

along the length of his spine. He knew, with every essence of his being, that when the darkness appeared, he would be the only thing standing between it and Liz's life.

He just hoped to hell he would be enough.

Chapter 12

Twenty-four hours later, Liz was still waiting for a break in the Windsor case.

It was nearly noon when she returned to her office after meeting with an assistant DA to go over her upcoming testimony on a murder she'd worked while assigned to Homicide. Finding the door locked told her Sam had yet to make it back from the courthouse. If his search for legal documents that York filed years ago while in private law practice didn't lead to something, Liz wasn't sure they'd ever solve the murder.

While sliding her key in the lock, she heard heavy footsteps echoing along the basement's hallway. Glancing across her shoulder, she spotted the bull-necked civilian employee assigned to the P.D.'s mailroom.

"Got something for ya, Sergeant Scott."

"Thanks, Harold."

When Liz saw the return address on the thick mailing envelope, anticipation prickled over her skin. Nick Reynolds had worked the Windsor case thirty years ago. Since every homicide cop Liz had ever known routinely kept his or her own set of notes on each case, Liz had tracked down Reynolds in Alaska where he'd moved to be near his son. The retired detective confirmed he still had his file on the homicide, and would send her copies as soon as he dug it out of storage.

At last, she thought as she settled at her desk and opened the mailer.

Reynolds's loopy, unformed handwriting straggled across page after page of notes. By the time Liz finished reading what could only be described as crappy penmanship, her eyes throbbed.

The retired detective had included most of this information in his official reports. Still, he had made reference to some miscellaneous errands Geneviève had run the day she died that Liz didn't remember seeing in the homicide file. Nothing, however, jumped out at her as meaningful to help identify the woman's killer.

As expected, David York wasn't mentioned.

Disappointment twisted inside Liz's belly. Unless she and Sam found something soon, it looked like Geneviève would never get the justice she deserved.

Clipped to the back of Reynolds's notes was a

smaller envelope. The retired cop had added a note to Liz that he'd found several photos of Windsor that her mother had sent him a year after the murder.

Liz opened the envelope and slid out the photos. When she saw the one on top, she forgot all about her throbbing eyes.

It was the first color photo she'd seen of Geneviève. Her hair was a long fall of chestnut to her waist, her face equally striking. Her smile was compelling, her brown eyes as soft as dark caramels. But it wasn't the young woman's appearance that had Liz's breath catching.

It was the gold bracelet on her right wrist. Woven lovers' knots formed the wide cuff and a stone the color of hot flame was set into its center.

"Holy…"

"Holy, what?"

Liz jerked her chin up at the sound of Sam's voice. She watched him stride toward her desk, his gray gaze locked on her, his dark hair windblown from the crisp October breeze. For a split instant, she couldn't help but think there was something incredibly sexy about a man in his element, especially when that element was hunting a killer.

"Cow," she said, forcing her thoughts back on track. "Holy cow, Sam. Look at this picture of Geneviève Windsor."

He stood at the edge of her desk, studying the photo. Then his eyes snapped up to meet Liz's. "She's wearing the bracelet. I'll be damned."

"It's almost an exact match to the sketch J. D. Temple made of the one he stole from York's house. We can show Temple this picture to confirm it's the same bracelet." Liz shoved her long braid behind her shoulder. "This is it, Sam. The connection we need between York and Geneviève. Now we know why he didn't include the bracelet on the list of property Temple took. Because at some point York gave it to Geneviève. He knew that could link him with a murder victim."

"Which would be damn hard to get around." As he spoke, Sam tugged off his leather bomber jacket, tossed it over the chair at his worktable. "I found another connection while I was going through the archived records at the courthouse."

Feeling the hunting hormone flowing into her bloodstream, Liz leaned forward in her chair. She'd always savored the edgy anticipation that came when she scented a killer's trail. "What connection?"

"While York had his private law practice, he represented a couple of oil and gas firms. One of those was the company Windsor worked for."

Liz nodded while her cop mind worked on making the case against the now federal judge as strong as possible. "Just because York was the lawyer for the company where Geneviève worked doesn't prove they knew each other."

"I agree." Sam hitched a hip on the edge of Liz's desk. "But in my experience, oil company CEO's don't go to lawyers, the lawyers come to them. So I started the ball rolling on tracking down the CEO during the time Windsor worked there. If he's still alive and kicking, I'll set up an interview. If he's not, we need to find someone who worked close with him so there won't be any doubt that York and Geneviève had occasion to interact on the job."

"I have the name of a coworker who Geneviève was friendly with." Liz opened a file folder, started shuffling through the stack of reports. "I've left her one message but she hasn't—"

"Liz."

The sudden edge in Sam's voice had her looking up from the file. When she saw the grave look in his eyes, she felt her chest tighten. "What's wrong?"

"Have you looked at the rest of these photos of Geneviève?" He held them in one palm, fanned out like a hand of cards.

"Not yet. Why?"

"In this one, Geneviève has her right hand up, shading her eyes from the sun." Sam handed Liz the photo. "Check out the inside of her right wrist."

Shaken by his tone, Liz accepted the picture with an unsteady hand. The woman who met a violent death three decades before had a birthmark identical to hers.

"That can't be." Even to her own ears, her voice seemed to come from a long way off. "But it is," she added as she stared at the photo.

"We can write it off as a coincidence," Sam said quietly. "The same way I shrugged away the fact that

Geneviève's lover, Max Hogan, and I share an almost identical military record."

Liz laid the photo aside. "You know, if coincidences didn't exist, there wouldn't be a name for them."

"Just like reincarnation," Sam added.

Stunned, she could only stare at him. "Do you really believe I was Geneviève Windsor in a past life?" she managed after a moment. "And you were Max Hogan? That we're investigating our own murders?"

"I'm not sure what I believe anymore." Sam's steady gray eyes stayed locked with hers. "But here's a question. Do you think there are some things and some places that hold old memories in them? And the power that comes from them?"

The questions only added to the mass of confusion Liz found herself tangled in. "What are you talking about?"

"I told you about the edgy feeling that hit me the instant I touched the murder weapon. And think back to the day we went to the building where Geneviève lived. To your reaction when you tried to enter what had been her apartment."

Liz closed her eyes. For reasons she was at a loss to explain, she hadn't been able to return to the building since that day. "I touched the doorknob, and heat seared my palm."

"That apartment was on fire the night Geneviève died. She climbed out on the fire escape to try to get away from the flames and her killer."

"Who shot her with the Colt. Which was owned

by a guy who happened to have a replica of a bracelet cursed since medieval times because of some love triangle."

"Lovers who died together," Sam added. "Like Geneviève and the marine."

Liz lifted both hands, palms toward Sam, as if that would ward off his comment. "Look, I know you're used to this kind of stuff because of the conjuring that your grandmother and aunts and cousins do. But I have to tell you that I am now officially, totally freaked out."

"I'm not far behind you." Sam angled his chin. "I don't know what's going on, any more than you do, Liz. I'm just trying to cover all the bases."

"Fine." She glanced at her watch, then stood. "You'll have to do that without me this afternoon because I'm due in court to testify on that other case."

He rose off the desk. "While you're gone, I'll try to track down the oil company CEO."

"Even if you do find him, you need to hold off on interviewing him until after I have a chance to talk to my boss. We now have an official connection between a federal judge and a murder victim. I don't even want to think about how touchy this investigation just got."

"I'll hold off," Sam said.

Liz swung the strap of her tote bag over her shoulder, then paused. "Being a cop has taught me to respect things I don't understand. Because sometimes those things hold the key to a puzzle I need to solve. But this is the first time I've been personally involved in one of those puzzles. It's scary."

"I know." Sam reached out, squeezed her arm. "Any idea when you'll be done in court? We can go somewhere to talk this over. Try to figure things out."

Liz glanced at the calender on her desk. "We'll have to hold off on that until this evening. After I testify, I'm meeting Andrew. We have an appointment to empty the safe-deposit box we rented."

Still amazed that her life had transformed so totally in a matter of weeks, she dug into her tote. "Here's a key to my loft. Why don't you wait for me there?"

"All right." Instead of taking the key from her fingers, Sam enfolded her hand in his. "How about I cook you dinner tonight?"

As always, his touch sent her pulse into overdrive. "You didn't tell me you can cook."

His mouth quirked. "Sweetheart, this Louisiana boy is well known in dirty rice circles all over the country."

"I just bet you are."

His smile faded and his fingers tightened on hers. "Liz, it's possible we share a past. We know about the present. After we close the Windsor case, let's talk about the future."

She swallowed hard, surprised to find that she was more nervous now than she had been the night they slept together. It was a matter of control, she supposed. That night she had been so sure of the outcome when she'd led Sam up the stairs at her loft.

Right now, what lay ahead of them was a big, dark unknown.

"Do you think we have a future, Sam?" she asked quietly.

He looked at her intently. "I hope to hell we do."

While Liz parked her cruiser outside the county building, David York walked into his office in the federal courthouse.

After removing his black robe, the judge settled at his mahogany desk. As usual, his secretary had stacked his messages in the center of the blotter. York shuffled through them, his dark eyes narrowing when he came to one from Ricky Paavo.

As odious as he found Paavo, York immediately returned the call from the security guard at the county courthouse. Over the years, York had developed contacts who had access to all types of information, and he recognized the value of such. In Paavo's case, most of the gossip the man heard eventually turned out to be hard fact.

"You called?" York asked, not bothering identifying himself.

"Yeah, Judge, I was doing my rounds this morning and stopped by the archives office. There's this chick down there who's hot for me, and she told me something you might be interested in."

Although York doubted any woman would be "hot" for the ratty-faced rent-a-cop, he held his tongue.

"That depends on what the information pertains to."

"You."

York's spine stiffened against his leather chair. "I'm listening."

"Uh, first, I want to make sure our arrangement is still in place?"

"Of course," York replied. He and Paavo always dealt in cash. "I'll leave an envelope in the usual place."

"Swell. Well, the chick mentioned a cop stopped by this morning, wanting a run done on all legal documents you filed thirty years ago."

York felt his breathing shallow. "The officer's name?"

"Broussard. From somewhere in Louisiana."

A dull red haze of fury clouded York's vision.

"Thank you." With every word, York felt the coiling hatred inside him tighten. He hung up the phone with a snap, his teeth gritted tight to suppress the rage.

He had no idea what had prompted Broussard's search, nor did it matter. The point was, the warrior had found *something*.

York fisted his hands, hands that he had used to kill many times. His torment ran deep, through the decades and the lifetimes. He wanted peace. He wanted what had been promised to him. Elizabeth was *his*. Had always been his. Would always be. No matter what name she used.

And now that Broussard had checked into his past, the judge knew he could no longer keep his distance and wait to make his move. His involvement must now become intimate.

York sat motionless, his breathing shallow while he considered how best to finish what had been started centuries ago.

* * *

After Liz left for the courthouse, Sam managed to ward off thoughts that hammered at him while he worked on tracking down the former oil company CEO. He even kept his mind focused on the Windsor investigation while he sat at Liz's desk and reviewed the retired detective's notes.

That done, he fanned through the color photos of Geneviève Windsor. Finally he allowed his mind off the tight leash he'd kept it on and surrendered to those thoughts.

If he bought into the past life theory, it would explain his incessant feeling that somehow, someway he and Liz shared a past. And it could be the reason he'd grown up with her in his dreams. Then got hit by the bizarre feeling of destiny the day they'd met when he turned and saw Liz rushing toward him down the P.D.'s dim basement hallway.

Hell, he didn't know if there was a rational explanation for any of those things, Sam thought, scrubbing a hand over his face. Reincarnation would explain their uncanny connection but he wasn't sure it even existed. And he was less sure he could buy into the theory that he and Liz had lived—and died violently—in a past lifetime.

His eyes narrowed when his thoughts went to the tarot cards his grandmother had dealt while they talked on the phone. The Lovers. The Tower, with a destructive energy similar to death. The Knight of Swords, who used violence to get what he wanted.

Including murder.

The cop in him knew that disregarding any theory before all the facts were in could send an investigation so far off course that it never got back on track. So, he would keep an open mind. View the idea of reincarnation as just one more lead to work with.

The phone rang, jerking Sam's thoughts back. Hoping the call was a lead to the oil company CEO, he grabbed the receiver. And immediately recognized the voice of the lab tech to whom he'd submitted the hors d'oeuvres pick with York's DNA.

"What can you tell me?" Sam asked.

"The DNA on the pick matches the DNA profile from the tissue and blood found inside the Colt."

Sam's pulse thudded hard. "How sure are you?"

"Ninety-nine point nine percent positive both samples came from the same person."

Savage satisfaction shot through Sam as he ended the call. Finding York's DNA inside the Colt didn't prove the judge killed Geneviève Windsor. But it did establish he'd fired the murder weapon at some point. That, along with the legal documents that linked York to the dead woman's job, were enough to pull York in for questioning. Sam could almost feel the noose tightening around the bastard's throat.

Wanting to update Liz, he dialed her cell. The call went to voice mail. He knew she'd have turned her phone off while testifying. Still, he couldn't help frowning when he checked his watch. It was just after four—by now she should have left the courthouse and headed to the bank to meet her ex-fiancé.

But maybe not. Something could have delayed her testimony, or it could have run long. Things like that were far from rare.

So why did he all of a sudden feel danger tripping through his blood?

Not bothering to wait for an answer, he shoved out of his chair and headed out of the office.

Divvying up the contents of a safe-deposit box with the man she had once believed she would spend the rest of her life with had put knots in Liz's stomach.

That Andrew had treated her with distant politeness while inside the bank was no surprise. After all, she had left the man standing at the altar twice. And been unable to explain the reason why to him, or herself.

Now, it seemed, fate had been at work. Fate, in the form of a recovered murder weapon that had brought Sam into her life.

Having tumbled into love so quickly, so deeply, felt almost surreal. Yet as she watched Andrew's impeccably maintained Mercedes turn out of the bank's parking lot, a sense of rightness settled over her.

Sam was the one. The only one.

And by now he should be at her loft, cooking her dinner.

Sometimes it was good to let fate take you by the hand, Liz decided, her mouth curving.

She unlocked the door to her cruiser and pulled it open. As she tossed her leather tote onto the passenger seat, she felt a sharp prick against the side of her neck.

"All I have to do is press, just a little," a low voice murmured. "The knife will slice into your carotid and you'll bleed out in minutes."

Liz recognized York's voice at the same instant she felt the sting against her arm. Her vision blurred. Her legs turned to rubber.

"Let me help you into the car," he said softly.

An hour and a half after leaving the cold case office, Sam pushed through the bank's revolving door. He'd missed Liz at the courthouse, then spent precious time tracking down Allie Fielding—who had to touch base with Claire Castle—to find out the name of the bank where Liz and her ex-fiancé had their safe-deposit box.

Just inside the door, Sam spotted a uniformed, off-duty OCPD cop with a gray crewcut and hard eyes working security. Flashing his badge, Sam asked if the cop had seen Sergeant Scott.

"She was here," he confirmed. "Later, I saw her walk out with the same guy who'd been waiting for her over by the safe-deposit box desk. About five minutes after that, I spotted them driving off in her cruiser, headed eastbound."

"They drove off *together?*" Sam asked.

"Guess so." The cop raised a shoulder. "There were two people in the cruiser."

Frowning, Sam went out the revolving door, paused on the sidewalk and again tried Liz's cell. When the call went to voice mail, he stabbed a hand through his hair.

He had no doubt that Liz and Andrew's romantic relationship was over. Still, they might have gone somewhere else together because of other business they needed to wrap up. But that didn't explain why she wasn't answering her phone.

Nor did it quell the dread whispering through Sam's veins. Standing there in the waning afternoon sunlight, he was aware of a heaviness to the air that felt ominous. Menacing.

He placed another call to Allie Fielding. Five minutes later, she phoned him back.

"I just talked to Andrew," she said. "He walked out of the bank with Liz, but then drove off in his own car. They weren't parked near each other, so he didn't see her get into her cruiser. Or who she was with."

Sam tightened his grip on the phone. All of his instincts told him the man she'd driven off with was York.

"Sam, what's going on?" Allie asked. "Has something happened to Liz?"

The concern for her friend was ripe in Allie's voice, but he didn't address it. Just as he couldn't bear to acknowledge the sheet of ice that encased his heart.

"I'm hoping everything's fine," he said before ending the call.

In the next instant, he pictured himself reaching out for Liz, but he was too late to stop her from falling into a bottomless, dark abyss. The marrow-deep terror shooting through his veins told Sam that what he had just experienced wasn't some imaginary vision. It was real. *It had happened before.*

Was going to happen again.

His pulse pounding with the certainty that the window of time he had to find Liz was closing fast, he dashed back into the bank. And hoped to hell there was a security camera aimed at the parking lot.

Liz woke to a world that was fuzzy and disjointed. Had she been in an accident? She remembered driving—no, no, *she* hadn't been driving. Someone else was behind the wheel. But they'd been in her cruiser....

She needed to wake up, but her eyes refused to open and nausea rolled in her stomach. A concussion, she thought hazily. Was that why she felt sick? Why her head throbbed? How...the parking lot. She recalled standing at her cruiser with the door open, watching Andrew drive away from the bank. Then she felt the knife against her throat. The sting of a needle in her arm an instant before her vision blurred.

That memory started the nausea swirling inside her with a vengeance. Fingers of fear slid over her skin. Digging down for strength, she forced her eyes open.

The room was small and dim, the door closed, the single window covered with a blind. The white walls were bare, the only furniture the double bed on which she lay. Weak light filtering through the blind told her it was still day. But her sense of time was distorted, and she had no idea which day.

She tried to check her watch, but discovered her left wrist wouldn't move.

When she jerked her head sideways, panic rushed

in. She was handcuffed to the center of the bed's brass headboard!

York. The realization came crashing in on her. Whatever he'd injected her with had hit her like a sledgehammer. With her head swimming and her legs turning to rubber, she'd been powerless to resist when he shoved her into the cruiser and over into the passenger seat.

She had a vague memory of York driving them somewhere while her mind screamed in protest. Of him getting her out the passenger door. Despite anger, fear and training, she'd been powerless to resist as he wrapped an arm around her to prop her up and walk her toward a brick building. If anyone saw them they would have assumed she'd been drunk….

Geneviève's building! Liz swallowed hard while struggling to snap back. She remembered now, York jostling her into the elevator, the way the smell of fresh paint had made her stomach turn over. And then everything had gone black, as if she had stepped off the rim of a canyon in the middle of the night.

Since he'd brought her to this building, she was most likely in Geneviève's bedroom. Liz's gaze shot to the window. It was through there that the woman had crawled onto the fire escape in an attempt to flee York before he shot her.

Scrambling into a sitting position, Liz jerked on the cuffs, and muttered a curse when she recognized them as her own. Craning her neck, she swept her gaze across the room. There was no sign of her tote bag, which held a handcuff key, her phone, her badge. Her .357 automatic.

With the mists moving back to the corners of her mind, she angled her wrist. According to her watch, only three hours had passed since York grabbed her. Was Sam still at her loft, keeping the dinner he'd cooked warm? Was he concerned she hadn't yet shown up, or did he think she was still with Andrew?

"Sam." She whispered his name, her pulse racing in her throat. He'd been adamant he needed to protect her from York. Shield her. And all along, she'd insisted she could take care of herself.

Now, all she could do was hope to hell she was right.

Just then, the door swung open and York stepped into the room. He was dressed in a tailored black suit, his silver hair looking rigorously brushed, his chin smoothly shaven. He looked nothing like a kidnapper and everything like a distinguished jurist on his way to a social engagement.

"Ah, you're awake," he said smoothly. "I trust the drug hasn't left you feeling too ill?"

She gave him the hard-eyed stare she had used on countless suspects over the years. "Unlock these cuffs and let me go. Otherwise, you'll spend the rest of your life in a cage."

His dark eyes were cool, very cool, as his gaze slid over her. "My dear Elizabeth, I'm not concerned about the immediate future. We're here to rectify the wrong you did to me in the past."

"I'd rather talk about the wrong you did to Geneviève Windsor and Max Hogan."

"Ah, so you do know." York tipped his head. "I wouldn't have been forced to do that if you had obeyed your father."

Liz blinked. "*My father?* You've got me confused with someone else, York. I got left in a self-service laundry when I was a week old. No one knows who my father is."

"Not in *this* lifetime. We've lived through many, the three of us."

Holy hell, Liz thought, struggling for calm. When she and Sam had theorized about reincarnation, it had been just that—a theory. To hear York talk, it sounded like he'd bought into the entire concept.

She kept her gaze on him while she strained to hear the sound of other people. But the absolute silence around them told her the building was as vacant now as it had been when she and Sam visited it weeks ago. Screaming for help would be futile. So, she had to keep York talking while she figured out a way to get him close enough so she could land a crippling kick.

"The three of us?" she prodded.

"You, myself and the man who now calls himself Broussard."

"Okay, let's say you know what you're talking about. Exactly how did I disobey my father?"

"He betrothed you to me when you were very young. Too young to consummate the union." While he spoke, York slipped his hand into his pocket. "I had this blessed, and gave it to you as my pledge that I would wait for you."

Liz's chest tightened when she saw the bracelet in his palm. The wide, woven band gleamed gold and the red opal in its center shimmered like leaping flames.

"You're the one who didn't wait," York continued as he eased toward the bed. "You fell in love with the landless son of a minor baron and begged your father to release you from the betrothal. But he was a man of honor and refused. He recognized that I was a much better husband for you in that I possessed lands, wealth."

York's expression had turned malicious and his voice sounded centuries old. "You were my property. By law. By the church. Despite that, your lover challenged me in a tourney."

Liz struggled to control her breathing while her fisted fingers dug crescents into her palms. This guy had to be crazy. Psycho ward crazy.

"Look, York, whatever happened back then or didn't happen doesn't matter. You need to focus on now."

"I assure you, Elizabeth, I am very focused." He extended his arm, the bracelet in his palm. "When you gave this to your lover, the blessing bestowed on it became a curse. You must wear it while swearing your love for me. Only then will the curse be broken."

"Stay away from me, you sick—"

His hand whipped out with the speed of a striking snake and locked on her right wrist. "The day you came to my chambers the building was warm. You shoved up your sleeves and I saw my mark. *My mark, Elizabeth. You are mine. Mine for all time."*

Liz attempted to jerk from his hold, but his fingers gripped her arm like steel spikes. Then he clamped the bracelet on her wrist, and she felt a jolt.

The world around her took on another dimension. Colors that had no names and unidentifiable sounds flashed before her eyes. A wave of sensation swept through her. The gold cuff seemed to come alive, warming her flesh beneath it while faint vibrations from it flowed up her arm and toward her heart.

She would give the bracelet to him, she thought as she felt herself being drawn through the dark, swirling tunnel of an endless past. She would give everything she had, everything she was to keep the man she loved safe.

All at once she and Sam stood before a castle of forbidding gray stone that towered above a raging sea. She was clad in a hooded cloak, a sword hung at his side.

"I have to marry him," she shouted over the wind that blew like a wrath across the cliffs. "There's no other way."

"There is *a way." Sam swept her into his arms, his hand fisting into her long hair. "I've challenged him for you."*

The fierceness in his eyes told her he wouldn't back down. "Take this." She jerked the bracelet off her wrist, shoved it into his hand. "Sell it. Buy armor that will protect you."

Suddenly, hoofbeats thundered toward them. She screamed as York leaped off his horse, sword drawn. Sam thrust her behind him. The air around them electrified when blade clashed against blade.

"No!" Desperate to save the man she loved, Liz threw herself at York. He thrust out a fist, shoved her, sending her stumbling over the craggy ground toward the cliff's edge.

Sam turned, straining to reach her. Just as their fingers brushed, York plunged his sword into Sam's back.

Screaming, she tumbled over the rocky ledge.

As Liz fell, a disjointed collage of lifetimes, of images and feelings swept over her. Sam in the uniform of a British army officer. Of herself wearing a ridiculous hoop skirt.

And, always, those lifetimes ended at York's murderous hands.

She struggled to make sense of the images in her mind while the cuff around her wrist seared her flesh like acid. But the pain sharpened her senses, focused them. And she saw York easing his way toward her like a hunter, his hand coming up slowly, gripping a silver automatic.

Like in my dream, Liz thought. Fear rose inside her as the dream merged with a terrifying reality.

"You are my property!" he shouted. "You will do as I command. Now, say it, Elizabeth. Swear your love for me."

Liz stared down the gun's barrel. He had shot

Geneviève. She had no doubt he would do the same to her.

With all of her strength, she kicked out at York.

At the last second he angled, deflecting the blow.

"Say it," he shouted, his eyes wild. "Swear it!"

Just then, the bedroom's door crashed violently inward as Sam burst in, weapon drawn.

York swiveled toward the door.

"Gun!" Liz shouted at the same instant Sam slammed his shoulder into York.

The force of the blow sent the judge flying backward, his body slamming against the wall.

Liz struggled against the cuff, her gaze locked on York. Panic gripped her when she realized the bastard still had the automatic clenched in his hand, aimed at Sam. His finger squeezed the trigger.

"Sam!"

The blast of gunfire swallowed the sound of her voice.

Seconds passed while fear stopped her heart, the silence around her pressing like fingers against her eardrums.

"Liz!"

She squeezed her eyes shut. Her heart started beating again. Sam was alive.

"I'm okay." She pushed up on her knees in time to see Sam approach York's body, which lay facedown to one side of the bed. With his own gun held steady, Sam kicked the automatic from York's hand, then pressed two fingers against his neck. That Sam made no move to handcuff the judge signified that he was dead.

Sam's face was a mask of concern as he rushed to her. "You're sure you're okay?"

"Yes." Still on her knees, she flung herself into his arms. "Yes."

Now that she was safe, icy terror bubbled up inside her. Her entire body shook and her pulse surged like a runaway train.

Liz eased back slightly. "You're fine, right? You didn't get hit?"

"I didn't get hit."

Just then, two strapping uniform cops stepped through the bedroom door, guns aimed.

Sam flashed his badge. "We need a handcuff key and an ambulance."

One of the cops bent over York's body while the other unlocked Liz's cuff.

"I don't need an ambulance," she protested while rubbing her wrist where the cuff had scraped her flesh raw.

Sam met her gaze with a hard gray one. "York injected you with something, right?"

"Right." She frowned. "How do you know that?"

"I'll explain later. Right now, you need to get checked out. Find out what he pumped into your system."

Liz thought about the visions she'd seen of her and Sam in past lifetimes. Had they been drug-induced hallucinations? Or had she and Sam actually lived those scenes?

"All right," she agreed after a moment. "I'll get checked out."

When Sam pressed a hand to her cheek, she felt a tremor deep inside him. "We'll talk later," he said quietly. "We need to talk."

Chapter 13

Hours later, Sam propped a thigh against Liz's desk and gave her a measuring look. Shadows of fatigue clung beneath her eyes and her cheeks were too pale for his liking. The bruises from the handcuffs that had circled her left wrist added to her aura of vulnerability.

This was the first time they'd been alone since paramedics swept her away from the apartment. An officer-involved shooting required the surrender of one's weapon, a half-dozen interviews and a mile of paperwork. Homicide, Internal Affairs and members of federal law enforcement had interviewed both him and Liz separately during the conduct of the investigation surrounding the death of Judge David York.

Sam felt no qualms over having killed the bastard. York had murdered Geneviève Windsor and Max Hogan. He'd drugged Liz, kidnapped her and held her at gunpoint. It didn't take a huge mental leap to figure York would have put a bullet in her.

Now, as he studied Liz, Sam felt all over again the chilling realization of how close he had come to losing her.

"I have a question," she said, looking up from the copy of the incident report that detailed her abduction. "How did you know York had me? And where he took me?"

"I didn't know at first. When you didn't answer your cell, I got worried. I tracked you to the bank. The cop working security there had spotted you driving off in your cruiser with some guy. I called Allie, and she phoned Andrew. After I knew you hadn't left with him, I had the sick feeling it was York. The cop ran the bank's security tape of the parking lot. It caught York seemingly helping you into your cruiser. At one point he angled his hand, and I caught sight of the syringe in his palm."

Despite the tight rawness in his throat, Sam kept his voice level. "The cop at the bank rallied the troops. While a patrol unit headed to York's house, I went to your loft. There was no sign of you at either place, so the only thing I could think to do was come back here."

Liz shot a puzzled look around the small basement office. "Did something here help you figure out where York had me?"

"Nothing specific. But I forced myself to just sit

here and think. I went over everything I knew about Geneviève Windor's murder. Then I asked myself, what if history *was* repeating itself? What if, on some cosmic level, you and Geneviève were the same person? Would you die again, the same way? At the same place?"

"The apartment I couldn't even set foot in," Liz said. "Where Geneviève had planned on meeting her marine. Then York showed up."

Sam nodded. "It was a hunch. Since I didn't have any other leads, I grabbed the keys to the building out of your desk and headed there. When I spotted your cruiser parked in the alley, I called dispatch and requested backup. But I didn't wait for them to arrive before I went in."

Liz gave him a faint smile while she slid her fingers over her bruised wrist. "I'm glad you didn't wait."

"And I'm damn glad you kicked York—his shot went high."

Because just the thought of how close that bullet had come to hitting Sam had Liz's stomach knotting, she picked up the report she'd finished reading and tapped its edges into alignment while she waited for her system to level.

But it wasn't going to level, she realized. At least not until she told Sam about what had happened while York had her.

Looking up, she met Sam's level gaze. "I need to tell you what I saw when York clamped the bracelet on my wrist." She took a deep breath. "At least I think I saw it."

"You *think?*" Sam asked, easing onto the desk.

"I don't know what kind of drug York gave me. It could have brought on hallucinations. Visions."

"Okay," Sam said softly. "Tell me what you saw."

"Different lifetimes. Us, together in different lifetimes. In the first, we were standing outside a castle. I was dressed in a cloak, you carried a sword."

Sam narrowed his eyes. "A cloak and a sword," he repeated.

Liz held up a hand. "Just let me get this out."

"All right."

"I'd been promised to York, but it was you I wanted," she continued. "You challenged him for me. I gave you the bracelet, begged you to sell it and buy stronger armor. York shoved me toward the cliffs. You tried to save me, but he stabbed you in the back. I fell."

Liz closed her eyes. She could still feel herself plunging into the churning sea below the cliffs.

"I died," she said after a moment. "Then flashes of other lifetimes blipped through my head. In them, you were always an officer of some sort, a protector. York was always there. And each time he killed us."

"And we're back to wondering about the reincarnation theory," Sam said, his gray eyes somber.

"Even York talked about it, like he was a firm believer." Liz huffed out a breath. "So, if he's right, does that mean we should expect him to show up again in X number of years?"

"Not a pleasant thought." Sam crossed his arms over

his chest. "When York talked about reincarnation, what did you think? As a cop, how did he strike you?"

"Crazy. A candidate for the psycho ward. I told him he needed to focus on now."

Suddenly Liz's body rang with the echoes of her ordeal. She felt emptied out and exhausted. She shoved the report into a folder, then rose.

"Think we should take that advice, too?" Sam asked. "Put everything about the past, real or imagined, aside and focus on now?"

"I don't know what to think," she shot back as each individual pulse point in her body began to throb in frustration. "It wasn't that long ago I had this nice, organized life with my future planned out. I knew what I wanted. Where I was headed. Then all of a sudden, the dreams started and I thought I was going nuts."

She swept her hand in Sam's direction. "Then you showed up and that kicked things into an out-of-control spiral. Everything changed. My *life* changed so much that I don't recognize it anymore."

She shoved her chair against her desk while blinking furiously to hold back a sudden rush of tears. "I don't even know if what's between us is real. Is what I feel for you real? Or is it some psychic phenomenon caused by a shift in the planets?"

The tears that glistened in her eyes and clogged her voice put a hitch in Sam's gut. He had no clue if they'd spent past lifetimes together. No idea if the visions they'd both experienced were real. At this point, he didn't care. All he cared about was claiming this intriguing, compelling woman for this lifetime.

Leaning, he snagged her hands, tugged her around the chair to stand before him. "How about I tell you how I feel? And how I know what's between us is real?"

She didn't say anything, just nodded.

"When I met Tanya, I think part of the reason I fell so hard for her was that I *wanted* to fall hard. I was ready to find someone. Ready to settle down. I convinced myself I was in love and wouldn't listen when my grandmother told me I'd hooked up with the wrong woman. The bottom line was, I wanted to want Tanya."

While he talked, Sam skimmed his thumbs across Liz's knuckles. "But I realize now, that what I felt for her wasn't real. I cared about her, sure. But not enough. I'll always regret that I couldn't be what she needed to be happy. And I'll never stop feeling guilt for what happened to her."

He tightened his fingers on Liz's. "When you and I met, I didn't want to feel anything. I didn't trust myself not to screw up another relationship, and the last thing I wanted was to care about you." He raised a shoulder. "What I wanted didn't seem to matter because you took hold of my heart and I fell in love."

Her lips trembled. "And all I wanted was to get my life back on track. I didn't want to care about you, either."

He shifted onto the desk, bringing her closer until she stood between his thighs. "Does that mean you do care?"

She nodded. "I kept telling myself I hadn't known you long enough, that it was too soon to love you. But then there were times when I felt like I'd known you forever." She shook her head. "All along, something inside of me knew that what I felt for you was right. That being with you was right. Is right."

"And when it is, you don't have to look for the reasons." Raising a hand, he curled his palm around the back of her neck. Slowly he brought her mouth to his and savored her warm, ripe taste that charged through his system.

Minutes—or maybe hours later—she locked a hand on his shoulder and leaned back. Her eyes were big and dazed. "Maybe we've known each other longer than we think," she breathed. "Maybe we were born loving each other."

"That's a possibility." He nipped his teeth along her jaw and grinned when a moan rose in her throat. "Either way, life's too short for us to waste time wondering about things we'll never know for sure."

He dipped a finger beneath the neckline of her sweater, traced the hollow beneath her collarbone.

"So, Sergeant Scott, those bruises on your wrist must be pretty painful. Think you can call your captain and arrange to take some sick leave?"

"What do you have in mind, Detective Broussard?" Her body trembled against his touch.

"I was headed to Colorado when you waylaid me. There's a cabin there with a full pantry and a stocked bar."

Liz narrowed her eyes. "*I* waylaid *you?*"

His mouth curved. "Something like that. Bottom line is, I'm under orders from my lieutenant to take time away from work. I still need to do that. Want to pack a bag and go with me?"

Liz cupped her palm against his cheek. "It just hit me that I've come face-to-face with the man of my dreams. I love you, Sam."

Relishing the swift kick of joy, he pulled her closer. Her body molded against his, warm and soft. Perfect fit, he thought.

"I love you," he murmured. "Forever."

* * * * *

Don't miss THE REDEMPTION OF RAFE DIAZ,
the next thrilling chapter in Maggie Price's
new Silhouette Romantic Suspense miniseries
DATES WITH DESTINY
Coming soon, wherever Silhouette Books are sold.

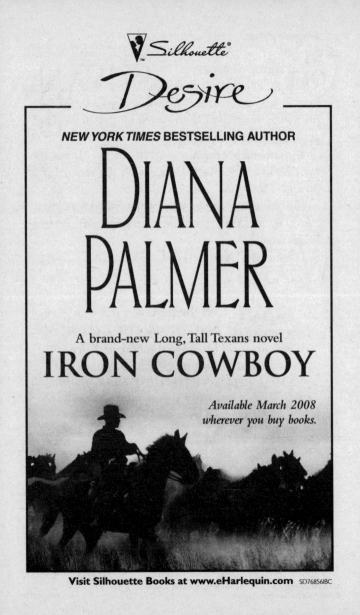

NEW YORK TIMES BESTSELLING AUTHOR

DIANA PALMER

A brand-new Long, Tall Texans novel

IRON COWBOY

Available March 2008
wherever you buy books.

Visit Silhouette Books at www.eHarlequin.com SD76856IBC

$1.00 OFF

The bestselling Lakeshore Chronicles continue with *Snowfall at Willow Lake*, a story of what comes after a woman survives an unspeakable horror and finds her way home, to healing and redemption and a new chance at happiness.

SUSAN WIGGS

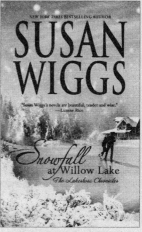

NEW YORK TIMES BESTSELLING AUTHOR

SUSAN WIGGS

"Susan Wiggs's novels are beautiful, tender and wise."
—Luanne Rice

Snowfall at Willow Lake
The Lakeshore Chronicles

On sale February 2008!

SAVE $1.00 off the purchase price of **SNOWFALL AT WILLOW LAKE** by Susan Wiggs.

Offer valid from February 1, 2008, to April 30, 2008.
Redeemable at participating retail outlets. Limit one coupon per purchase.

52608168

Canadian Retailers: Harlequin Enterprises Limited will pay the face value of this coupon plus 10.25¢ if submitted by customer for this product only. Any other use constitutes fraud. Coupon is nonassignable. Void if taxed, prohibited or restricted by law. Consumer must pay any government taxes. Void if copied. Nielsen Clearing House ("NCH") customers submit coupons and proof of sales to Harlequin Enterprises Limited, P.O. Box 3000, Saint John, N.B. E2L 4L3, Canada. Non-NCH retailer—for reimbursement submit coupons and proof of sales directly to Harlequin Enterprises Limited, Retail Marketing Department, 225 Duncan Mill Rd., Don Mills, Ontario M3B 3K9, Canada.

5 65373 00076 2 (8100) 0 11463

U.S. Retailers: Harlequin Enterprises Limited will pay the face value of this coupon plus 8¢ if submitted by customer for this product only. Any other use constitutes fraud. Coupon is nonassignable. Void if taxed, prohibited or restricted by law. Consumer must pay any government taxes. Void if copied. For reimbursement submit coupons and proof of sales directly to Harlequin Enterprises Limited, P.O. Box 880478, El Paso, TX 88588-0478, U.S.A. Cash value 1/100 cents.

® and TM are trademarks owned and used by the trademark owner and/or its licensee.
© 2008 Harlequin Enterprises Limited

MSW2493CPN

In the first of this emotional Mediterranean Dads duet,
nanny Julie is whisked away to a palatial Italian villa,
but she feels completely out of place in Massimo's
glamorous world. Her biggest challenge, though, is
ignoring her attraction to the brooding tycoon.

Look for

The Italian Tycoon
and the Nanny

by Rebecca Winters

in March wherever you buy books.

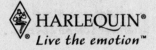

www.eHarlequin.com

HR17500

◆ HARLEQUIN®

INTRIGUE®

THRILLER—
**Heart-pounding romance and suspense
that will thrill you long into the night....**

Experience the new THRILLER miniseries
beginning in March with:

WYOMING
MANHUNT

BY

ANN VOSS
PETERSON

Riding horseback through the Wyoming wilderness
was supposed to be the trip of a lifetime for
Shanna Clarke. Instead she finds herself running
for her life. Only rancher Jace Lantry can
help her find justice—and serve revenge.

*Available in March
wherever you buy books.*

www.eHarlequin.com   HI69316

Romantic

SUSPENSE

COMING NEXT MONTH

#1503 A DOCTOR'S SECRET—Marie Ferrarella
The Doctors Pulaski
Dr. Tania Pulaski vows never to get involved with a patient. Then Jesse
Steele enters her ER. Although he's strong and attractive, she hesitates
taking things to the next level…until someone starts stalking her and
she must trust the one man who can help her.

#1504 THE REBEL PRINCE—Nina Bruhns
Serenity Woodson knows the charismatic and sexy man who's been
helping her aunt must be a con man. Then she learns the incredible
truth—Carch Sunstryker is a prince from another planet, on a mission
to Earth that may save his kingdom. Loving him would be insanity—
but neither can resist the intense attraction that could destroy them
both.

#1505 THE HEART OF A RENEGADE—Loreth Anne White
Shadow Soldiers
After Luke Stone fails to protect his wife and unborn child, he refuses
to take on another bodyguard assignment. But when he becomes the
only man who can protect foreign correspondent Jessica Chan from
death, he faces the biggest challenge of his life...because being so close
to Jessica threatens to break his defenses.

#1506 OPERATION: RESCUE—Anne Woodard
Derrick Marx will do anything to rescue his brother from the terrorists
holding him captive, including kidnapping the reclusive botanist whose
knowledge of the jungle is the key to his success. Against her will,
Elizabeth Bradshaw leads Derrick through the jungle, but quickly finds
the forced intimacy is more dangerous
than the terrorists themselves.

SRSCNM0208